NUDIBRANCHIA

NUDIBRANCHIA

or

"All Changed, Changed Utterly:
A Terrible Beauty is Born"
—W. B. Yeats
"Easter, 1917"

Sam Eisenstein

RED HEN PRESS ❦ LOS ANGELES

Nudibranchia

Copyright © 2003 by Sam Eisenstein

All Rights Reserved

No part of this book may be used or reproduced in any manner whatever without the prior written permission of both the publisher and author.

Book and cover design by Mark E. Cull

ISBN 1-888996-75-7

Library of Congress Catalog Card Number 20031121311

The City of Los Angeles Cultural Affairs Department,
California Arts Council and
the Los Angeles County Arts Commision
partially support Red Hen Press.

Manufactured in Canada

First Edition

Red Hen Press
www.redhen.org

All thanks to Caroline Widener
for sheltering me during a summer of fearful exile.

NUDIBRANCHIA

When I was growing up I felt that I had no audience.
No one wanted to listen to me. I thought, if you do not
want to listen to my voice at least I can force you to
listen to my song.
> —Benjamin Wilkomirski,
> in an interview with Louise Steinman
> *Los Angeles Times*, January 7, 1997

How in the name of Almighty Darwin
could such things evolve?
> —Chair

Dr. Lloyd

When Adrianna first came to the department I overlooked her for several weeks, mistaking her for one of our few remaining bright students. She was dark, ridiculously slender, skinny really, skeletal almost. Upon being introduced: "This is Adrianna Sealianthropa"—that's what it sounded like anyway—my first words, I'm not in English as Second Language, were, "Ah, so what we have here is a sea creature sleek with secretions from the bottom of the sea in process of transformation to—" "Anthropos?" she smiled, full of teeth, out of brightly painted wide lips, reminiscent of Africa modified by centuries in Asia, "not quite, not so far as I'm concerned. I am, you should know immediately, not interested in transformation so much as transmigration." "Of souls, do you mean? Oh, we don't have much of that here, as you'll find out in a blessed hurry." "Or slurry?" she smiled again, and immediately her forehead curled an apology. "Oh, forgive me, Dr. Lloyd, I have heard from everyone you love to play with words and so—" "Quite so, quite so," I interrupted, feeling familiar ruthless heart-lurching within, a breathless fatal attrition of judgment. Signaling the start of ploy, tiles on board before I noticed, which meant I lost at least two turns. Delicious, however, that she cared enough to decimate, ravish me before I even knew her entire name. Maybe I would never learn it, this was the chance given after I thought all such chances were over with, to jump into darkness. Appropriate, her skin more than milk chocolate, cooking chocolate, businesslike ready to flavor with itself every ingredient. Was she going to try to enter the Department masquerading Black? "Maybe I should, but it feels so hypocritical." "Perhaps also Lesbian and Jewish, not to mention disabled? Any Thalidomide in your family tree?" "Thalid—what?" "Ah, you-are-so-young! Flippers, Adrianna, vestigial extremities, like cranial organs in our students." She looked at me disapproving for the first time. It was delicious. I was flogged. I imagined flogging by her. So religious, I soon found, charismatic in fact, speaking, hearing in tongues, auras, all that quackery, but delicious. Flogging took root in my mind because she exuded it, I was sure. She wanted it, wanted to be not here but in the desert scourged by scorpions, forcibly taken like St. Catherine, another brute at every turn of the wheel. I took a look at her, sparse in front, royally endowed in rear parts. Steatopygia, relic no doubt of regal African background, where her people stored jewel-like water, more precious than gold during dry years, blood protected from drying out, stored in the ass, more than a handful. I'm sure our African students did not fail to notice, I watched their reactions as she strode the halls, they were ashamed of their eyes falling around her like chains, so that she dragged by the time she reached the bathroom. I flung them off, one after the other to their complete bewilderment, and when their eyes left her they found mine fiercely burning, possessive. Bewildered, they shambled away, insulted and wounded, not sure where to fix blame. All in the moment before the Chair turned, social duty done. In my head I said to her, immediately I leave that woman I live with, what difference our decades together, before your very birth, Adrianna, mere premonitory for this, don't you agree? Isn't this it? Tell me this is it. Instead, I said, "What does it mean to be Charismatic and Catholic? It seems to me contradictory in terms, a slap in the face of the primate, I don't mean the monkey," laughing, showing my teeth carefully, hiding gaps—nothing more off-putting than loss of teeth, much worse than hair, mere nothing. But teeth—rending, rendering, buttress for kissing. And without kissing, what? I gloamed Adrianna's lips, prehensile on me, I dared not imagine where, not yet. I was lost swooning. She would take it as conversion, perhaps it was. Electric from alternating to direct current. She was frightened, I could tell, she was reading me. She offered back my pawns, I wouldn't take them. The game's afoot! I shouted jovial as a knight up against her bishop. Aslant, I pranced on the board, her stately frocked hooded cleric looked through me as I sweated in armor, as willing to be killed as convert. I am wounded, Adrianna, look at me sweltering cut in the groin by cruelly uncaring Saracen metal, life blood spitting, substitute for semen meant for your hand. Wash me, take me on your arm, hold me up to incongruously smiling rays of diminishing suns. "Have you been in this office long?" She looked around, askance, I saw with her eyes. Dirty, shabby! If only I hadn't lost that job in a real school she would have happened while I was younger, with firmer thoughts and hamstrings. "Dirty, yes, but mine own. I've been here forever, spider in this corner, ready to pounce on you, not to eat but wrap—do you know Charlotte's Web?—for the odd rainy day. Protein on the hoof, you know, better than gorging all at once." "They told me you talk nonsense, but I like it, I like the way you talk nonsense." "My way of testifying," I blushed, moved beyond anything, "hand held over male organ," perhaps in time, yours too, Beloved— who were classical Adriannas? For me to look it up she had to leave the office, shoot her a note—no, too dangerous, suppose she used it to flay me, take my job, who cares? Male never spins webs, fool! "His Holiness the Pope is fond of Charismatics," she murmured. "His Holiness, the very idea, when nobody knows how to build the bridge from virginity to purity, let alone to that, what a sham, how ramshackle your fidelity." I saw Adrianna fling herself into a boat bound for the next ant-hill. "Farewell, you had your chance," she shouted, still smiling, forgiving where I aimed to want her to love. "Her name's Adrianna," the Chair said, "you'll need to make room for her in here, is that all right with you?" Sure, for a few months and then like mummied ventricles dry up, blow away, vanish leaving behind only slime trails of unstoppered perfume of desire for desire.

Adrianna

I came from bullrushes smiling to placate the Egyptian-sort I knew would be there after Father and Mother—shushing each other with that certain smile on their lips—put finishing touches on me.

I was constituted from dirt of dirt, a slime slurry of spiny serpents, a blush of ground-up egg sulphur still upon them. Even when done with me, each parent kept tender hold of the other explaining by gesture to the other what was still amiss. When at last as from a proscenium I was unleashed to spring onto the apron of the Theatre of Life, I was already over-ready, perhaps burdened by so much beauty, which explains my slight smile—this is not condescension but rather apology for too much perfection—because that is how I was sent forth, on this little rushing, this canasta of my body, into the world, dazed crushed by accumulated atmospheres of entry.

As soon as I know someone at all, I make free to lay my aristocratic fingers over his lips to shush him, make him still, encouraging him to seal up that deepest of orifices to render it again virgin, while he wondering, deep in neonateness, what long fleshy thing so hot and cool at once caresses him, fondles his lips, foothills to the temple.

I knew Dr. Lloyd was apt for pupilhood, rancid with words, every crack and cranny filled with nay-saying, so putrid his smell rolled out of even new books I opened in his absence in that office he had occupied more years than Dearest Jesus was allowed life.

He chittered like an ape, prehensile tail quivering over me ready to dart down, then imagining himself a scorpion ready to plunge paralyzing stinger into the place where his hungry eyes lingered as I turned stooping to pick up some filth, I caught him as he made lariat of his tongue, thus assuring my continuity in the Department.

I closed eyes perfect and secure in the knowledge I would as always be enabled to read the Lord's guidance etched on the undersides of my lids. I paled as much as chocolate frappe skin allows at the message, as ever unambiguous. I was to unsteel myself to become so soft as to allow, aid and abet Dr. Lloyd to enter me, where and whatsoever he should wish, as he had rank—obviously in the first moment so demonstrated his desire on my person. But, Lord—I speak directly—Dr. Lloyd may be unprincipled but also disciplined, even if only by a devil. "That's OK," saideth the Lord, "you'll just have to tempt and lead him, remember rancid, etc." I pleaded with the Lord to spare me this unfolding humiliation, but I knew it was no good once His word was cut into my flesh, and I saw pale palimpsest of Father and Mother nodding smiling urging.

I dared sulk. This involved looking in the mirror, otherwise forbidden. A handmaiden does not regard her posterior, but Lord! You could have allowed flesh to migrate north and west, vouchsafed one shimmy that might have settled flesh upon my chest. If I am to stroll among Children of Cain, why not tender me one tiny little disguise? The way I am, they notice me going but not coming, thus have I no way to protect myself. Did You not foresee things when You formed me? I am humbled, my Lord, You knewest best. Is the plan to allow me to test them all, undetected in my mission by the mulish male multitude? But am I to meet my end (no pun, Lord!) by way of an unseen unheard axe cutting me in twain? Is this to be mine only parturition, not fruitful like other daughters of Adam spawning their tribe as easily as biting into a pear?

Whatever You decree for me, O Lord, with that am I well satisfied.

Yet—with Dr. Lloyd? This *is* sore travail.

The Secret-ary

I take my name seriously. It was given me, I didn't seek it out, it found me. So there it stands, like a righteous wall, separating good from bad, and it didn't take long for me to find out which was which.

Professor Lloyd—what kind of name is that?—roars up on me like a truck that's lost its brakes, lights aglaring, but when he's about to knock me down, roll over my face with spiked tires, he comes to a complete stop, shudders a bit, turns his motor off, dims his lights and fades away utterly. He just stands there. "May I be of assistance to you in some way, Dr. Lloyd?" The first few times I asked real shaky before I knew what was coming. It was all a trick of course to make me nervous and lose composure because I see he does it with other women of color. I've caught him at it with our new long-term sub, Adrianna.

She blushes, sweet thing, so I just want to squeeze her face up in my bosoms. She knows it, smiles that wide red smile with just perfection of a little tongue peeping out from between the pearliest teeth God ever gave mortal woman. No matter how hard I watch, I never do get to see if it's red like her mouth. The tips of her teeth take on the red of her lips, so once I also took liberties, I held my breath and grabbed her nap and applied kleenex to the particular teeth frosted with lipstick. "Now there, Adrianna baby, nobody gonna fault your appearance, it's nigh perfect." And she blushed again, just like she does in front of Dr. Lloyd and some of the others, like Dr. Frank, for example, with his boastful talk about "submarining in the pleroma of the spirit," I'm *sure*, and "love shooting out like torpedoes streaking love and devotion." What is that pleroma I wondered, the dictionary in the office no use, I had to go clear to the library, drag out the big one. Here is what it says:

Pleresye, obs. form of PLEURISY.

‖ **Pleroma** (plĭrōŭˈmă). [a. Gr. πλήρωμα that which fills, a complement, f. πληροῦν to make full, f. πλήρης full.]

1. Fullness, plenitude; **a.** in Gnostic theology, The spiritual universe as the abode of God and of the totality of the Divine powers and emanations. **1765** MACLAINE tr. *Mosheim's Eccl. Hist.* I. II. II. v. (1833) 62/2 He placed in the *pleroma* (so the Gnostics called the habitation of the Deity) thirty æons. **1831-3** E. BURTON *Eccl. Hist.* iii. (1845) 58 One of these later emanations passed the boundaries of the Pleroma, which was the abode of the Deity, and there coming in contact with matter created the world. **1875** LIGHTFOOT *Comm. Col.* (1886) 100 For this totality [of the Divine powers] Gnostic teachers had a technical term, the *pleroma* or *plenitude*.

b. Used in reference to Colossians ii. 9, where the Eng. versions from 1388 have 'fullness': Ὅτι ἐν αὐτῷ κατοικεῖ πᾶν τὸ πλήρωμα τῆς θεότητος σωματικῶς: Wyclif 1388, 'For in hym dwellith bodilich al the fulnesse [1382 al plente, *Vulg.* plenitudo] of the Godhed'. **1875** LIGHTFOOT *Comm. Col.* 329 The ideal church is the pleroma of Christ, and the militant church must strive to become the pleroma. **1883** SCHAFF *Hist. Ch.* II. XII. xcv. 777 The pleroma of the Godhead resides in Christ corporeally: so the pleroma of Christ, the plenitude of his graces and energies, resides in the church as his body.

2. *Bot.* = PLEROME. *rare⁻*.
1890 in *Cent. Dict.* **1895** in *Syd. Soc. Lex.*
Hence **Pleromatic** (plĭˈromæ·tik) *a.*, pertaining to the pleroma.
1858 MAYNE *Expos. Lex.* 977/2 The *pleromatic kingdom* was the name given by Stockenstrand to the whole powers which animate the world and the stars which fill the celestial space. **1879** SCHAFF *Person of Christ* 56 The completeness or pleromatic fulness of the moral and religious character of Christ.

making about as much sense as Dr. Frank. "I'm on my way out. Cindy. About to rest my oar, going on eternal patrol. Cindy. I'm just waiting on final orders." "Well, you won't find them on *my* desk, Dr. Frank." "That's what neither of us knows, Ms Cindy, as a man of lifelong rectitude, nothing more has happened to me than a thickened prostate. Cindy."

He had to pause now and then because of shortness of breath. "Because of the rank air I breathed in the service of my country. Cindy. So you could be born, be here in the English Department. Lock your desk. Have privacy. No standing in line for the master of the house to tell you, 'bend over, woman, it's your turn.'" "Dr. Frank, I don't need to listen to this sort of thing." I flang him my haughty look. He wheezed some to cover his confusion. "I was just saying. I served when sub wasn't part of a sandwich. For your dignity. Cindy. I most utterly believe in your dignity. Really. In the forefront to acknowledge it." I have to admit he was first to point out my position as secret-ary. I *am* nerve-center of the Department, I am the recipient of every whispered clandestine word, I read every message before it goes in whatever box, all secrets filter through me. I order and I file them, mentally. I know them and collate them. I read the Department like a book, like a sitcom.

Nothing gets past me. For example, I happen to know when Dr. Frank will be required to retire. *He* doesn't, but I do. Fact: when he applied for convention grant money for two, it was not clear that he was married. Does that make Dr. Frank a godless hypocrite? Or what? If it does, he will certainly pay.

Anor

The creatures must cleanse, ingest, expel every four hours, more or less. I must be extremely careful to be appear to have the same necessities, albeit not precisely, as the resident genius in the Department demonstrates—exact duplication is suspect. Dr. Lloyd is eccentric, meaning wobbly, according to Webster's dictionary. Professor Lloyd—duplication of any first two letters is reminiscent of our custom at home, the better to produce a kind of hiss. Aside: I visit Ophidia in the zoo, but I have ascertained no possibility of communication exists with these examples of our far-flung but herein debased family, who, nonetheless, sensing something vaguely familiar, fling themselves about writhing, attempting with excited irritability to speak but sadly making no sense.

As you perceive, far-away Correspondents, I have more or less attached myself to Dr. Lloyd because he generally attracts the more interesting sort of faculty and student. I explain to all who will even pause to listen that I am vegetarian and may not as well wear leather as little as eat it, that is, meat, not its dried equivalents. I offer Dr. Lloyd and Adrianna little gifts I find from around this world at the 99¢ store. He is insanely fond of smallish canines made of porcelain. She adores holograms of the prophet Jesus on his knees praying surrounded by what appears to be igneous rock disciples. Chinese people are happy to export these trifles to the 99¢ store as well as firearms designed to kill a goodly number of people in one operation. A great deal of odd cooperation takes place here.

Adrianna suspects me of diabolic origin—close enough. Accordingly, she wishes to save me, a dangerous thing, as I am capable of incinerating her with a glance without warning if she suddenly becomes too annoying. Thus my plan is to find her constantly annoying, safer.

It is uncanny that with such a pathetically narrow factual base she is able to spread her evangelical arms wide enough to catch motes of truth, buzzing around me like a mosquito or bee. "I see through you, Devil!" she pronounces, yet smiling. "Anor! Bulim! Made-up names! Are the others all so stupid as not to see through you?" I wonder, is my disguise so transparent? I set to, to thicken epidermis, freeze cartilage into bone, though uncomfortable so rigid. She goes on: "And so thin, so supple, so—so, *me!*"

And then, inexplicably, Adrianna burst into tears, ran away into her office and slammed the door. This was serious. I easily insinuated myself through and confronted her, silent, arms crossed. I confess I made a pretty picture in the late afternoon sun, ruddy and seamless. "You patterned yourself on *me*," she sniffled, eyes still wet and catching a ray from the slanted sun, "You watched me on your way here, so you saw me naked, didn't you?" Her eyes glowed most unnaturally. "Didn't you? Admit it," and she advanced on me so suddenly I backed up into the door, flattening myself on it. Didn't she perceive, with her own weird kind of knowledge, that just in this moment I was helpless to protect myself, she could have rolled me up, thrown me out the window and made an end of me? "Yes, I know what I could do to you here and now, Anor. But nobody but you has even bothered to want to see me naked, with or without my will."

She sighed. "I suppose for the moment I must make do with an alien voyeur. But if you had actually touched me while modeling your earth body on mine, I would have to kill you. You do know that, don't you? And that goes for any time in the future. Did you know, monster, what actually you were looking at?"

I swayed my upper body, better to get a grip on dimensionality. In a flash I achieved girth and width. "Naturally. I know you are beautiful." She sighed, looking to mountains growing a few miles away north. "You lie, Anor, but not well enough. Oh, certainly, men look at me, but only when I wear breasts made from styrofoam, rubber and cotton. I do feel their eyes come to nest on me, but not really on me, but on the artificial elevations rising on my front. I ask you, Anor, can there be sustenance to a glance that dries and shrivels on non-living additions to my body? Am I destined by Lord Jesus to live on and on for this?" "Dry your eyes, Maiden, the time of your life will come. If you desire either of them, you have but to say so, I will ensnare Dr. Lloyd or Dr. Frank for you." "Stay out of my business, Anor. I don't know your actual mission here on earth, but Lord Jesus does not approve of it, for sure. Still, keep me posted about everything Cindy doesn't or can't. And please, make an attempt to look a little different from me." She giggled. "You're also growing breasts, for example, which I'm sure you've considered now that you see how held high in esteem I am now by the majority, will surely confuse this department enough that Chair may not consider you for a permanent position.

"Wouldn't it be fun to be in on the proceedings as they dance around the fact of their nervousness over frontal instability?" "They will hire me." "And what of me?" Adrianna flushed. "I shall expose you, Anor, devil's spawn! snatching by supernatural means the one probationary job, by all rights *my* job. Oh, why won't Jesus fight for me the way I fight for Him?" she said with more than a trace of bitterness, a far cry from her usual resignation. "Perhaps there will be here performed a marriage of convenience between heaven and hell," I snickered.

Then she had to do the four-hour thing—eat, pee, wash, drink, I don't know what because I lacked interest enough to follow her beyond the moment.

Chair

I live in hope and fear, Potala and Lhasa. Dr. Lloyd hasn't a clue why I am so tender with him, takes it for granted. If not for me, my interventions, how many times he would be banished to the outer reaches of empire to expire repining petitioning for reimposition of his green card, metaphorically speaking of course, since he is, at least for now, native-born.

"For your eyes only have I snared a great Nature program, Your Highness," he chants as I lope past his office hoping to avoid the magnetic draught, for naught. I am swept in, swinging as-yet hypothetical saffron robes safely above his sticky rubbish only to submit to his teasing wave of the PBS "Llamas I have Lloved," George Page narrating, whose voice is always better than mantra for induction of meditation or at least slumber, above my head, expecting me to leap for it. In truth, how can I resist, although never have I admitted to him (Dr. Lloyd not George Page) the truth that I am an aching lonely exile hidden inside the whirlwind of hyper-active service to the Department of English. "Not only that, but I happen to possess two tickets to a llama-hugging, babe," he cooes. "Even if they spit at you, it's better than nothing, right?" Yes! O holy beasts of my spiritual land of origin. Yes!

"Permission to come aboard!" I hear sung from the outer office as I stand, indecisive whether to accept the ticket held invitingly in front of my secretly-Mongolian nose by Dr. Lloyd—now what will he expect in return? I mentally stutter to imagine. He already holds every upper division class we offer in an increasingly bovine population, subject, as Adrianna puts it, to original Mad Cow Disease, not even the human equivalent. Oh, how witty she is, what a shame she is not more unbalanced—you know what I mean—though like her, I am vegetarian, even if I do not share her enthusiasm for Chow-Chow, a Chinese import—ugh!

Receiving no response, Dr. Frank put bosun's whistle to lips and blew into it so vigorously he surely endangered his very existence, besides forcing every insect within range to run for its life, thus keeping the place free from being over-run by vermin, even Dr. Lloyd's filthy office, but I'm sure he also threatened the very fabric of the universe as we know it. "Does a sailor have to shoot off depth charges around here to be noticed?" he croaked jovially, hugging both of us to his corpulence. Thus Dr. Lloyd and I found ourselves within nostrils' distance of each other, a not-unpleasant sensation, man-to-man, which in this society can only be managed in bathhouse or male-bonding group of thirty or more run by bad poets. "Give it to Dr. Frank," I managed weakly, desperate to retain amateur status, already much impaired, from the murmuring of innumerable temporaries who fan out each morning and evening to preach the faith of English to immigrants washed onto our shores while still wet and feverish with pale hope, before naive need solidifies to greed.

Lhasa and Potala! *My* keening need is such it is all I can do not to fling my foolish pathetic self into the arms of any visiting delegation of custodians, police cadets or plumbers, in wild momentary surmise they are at last disguised monks prepared to kidnap and carry me back swooning, more dead than alive, to be invested on the true throne that awaits me, now neglected and somber, until my spore or slime trail be tracked by spiritual bloodhounds to this place, this outpost, this slice of two-bit, fourth rate dusty Americana, my home, my frozen pizza.

"You'd come to regret it, old man," Dr. Lloyd said, eyeing me frankly, looking without permission into my vision. "Where shall we hunt, Dr. Lloyd?" whispered Dr. Frank, adding, "We must watch for rising bilge, as you well know," he said, kicking up little clouds of last year's exams with one steel-tipped combat boot. "What's this, never graded?" I didn't need to hear this, I sought refuge while they spoke in my own office with its panorama of different-colored pie charts indicating length and breadth of penetration by the English Department into the fabric of the whole, a veritable empire of the sun!

Dr. Frank

It was said of Abbot Agatho that for three years he carried a stone in his mouth until he learned to be silent. I listen and learn. I reside in deserts, a deserted father, a voiceless voice sent by wireless to the empyrean. I do not want to hear what the Secret-ary tells me, but she will burst if she does not speak. I listen as a public service. It was in Dr. Lloyd's office, the girl with short skirts went in. Cindy happened to have to sort papers just outside. That she heard more than saw she would be first to admit. As Dr. Lloyd sat fixated, the girl in front of him put her feet up on some books. "I'm sure he was looking straight up her dress, tiny as it was," Cindy said, "a crying shame. And if I hadn't cleared my throat, he might have been all over her, disgracing the Department and what-all, Dr. Frank, what are we coming to in this day-and-rage? And him sharing office space with that angel Adrianna, what if she had barged in on them just then, what would she think of us?" "She could cool her burning brow on your alabaster I mean basalt titties." "Dr. Frank, I rely on you to be a force for good around here and there you go saying a thing like that right to my face!" and she dabbed at said face with a tiny handkerchief though I detected a smile between the sheets. "I must apologize for my intemperate language. Cindy. So saddened am I that I don't know how to contain myself. We must keep vigil on Dr. Lloyd. We must up periscope and try to keep conning tower above water as long as possible, submerge when we must to maintain vigilance against the enemy." I looked around, a veritable telescope against iniquity, as though I truly expected to find that the enemy had sneaked into camp under our noses even as we spoke.

"Let me relate to you. Dear Cindy. What Abbot Pastor said: 'If you have a chest full of clothing and leave it for a long time, the clothing will rot inside it. It is the same with the thoughts in our heart. If we do not carry them out by physical action, after a long while they will spoil and turn bad.' What is Dr. Lloyd to do confronted with such a length of resilient flesh arched to his fingers, asking to be kneaded like dough, dusky thighs separated by startlingly white panties, pillowed by the secret dark curling gyrating hairs within, veritable dervishes, as in a trance of aching to expose themselves, blinding light rips across the elastic above as the gnarled hand of Dr. Lloyd descends to stroke, like a storm-tossed mariner in a frail leaking bark rowing and bailing for dear life."

Cindy sank suddenly into her posture-pedic desk chair, apparently overcome. "And so, we must simply put up with it?" she whispered. "We must mark the spot, release a buoy to keep our bearings," I responded heartily. "We are here standing duty for a purpose."

Anor

When the creatures are in doubt, they attempt to mate. I see them here around, teeth bare, saliva cascading down porous gums, absolutely unaware of their nature. That is actually one of things I find interesting about them—how amazing it is that they rarely question motive and motivation. They launch an offending one like a banana from its skin into the wilderness.

This is agreed. The offending one lies down to die, cooperatively. Then the others raise monuments to him or his organization. I seriously must examine if there exists something like this where I come from, among those who sent me here. Or is this actually exile, a wilderness? Am I truly being expected to obtain data or am I sent merely so as to cause no more upset, peacefully dying by pre-meditation? Also: am I really here or is all this implanted hallucination? I must not think this way, it will make me loony, truly. I have infected myself with the fantasy literature of this place, believing only what is irrational. Each of these people is no more than a swarm of particles, bacteria having agreed to settle for a few whiles, then in a dense cloud up and off they go. Oh, the people do not want to see them go, they speak of a soul like poor Adrianna. Everywhere, bacteria, but the people do not see them as kin, because they do not want to know they exist also in a particular niche, like the lowliest of slime animals. Amazingly, they subsist between invisible grinding boulders that age them, wear them down in a flash of our years, fall even as ash from a distant forest fire but allow themselves to know nothing—never. Is this punishment? In the midst of the most abandoned mating on their noses, eyelashes, skin, within their breathless clothing, they are alone, alone mateless, alone lonely.

I become more like them everyday, I am afraid. Will I stop eating and take on my name in truth? I must speak to Adrianna, but she avoids me. If she requires conversion, I will do anything, but to make her believe it? There's the rub.

Dr. Lloyd

Good thing Adrianna didn't come back then, good thing The Secretion did. My angel is working overtime. But Adrianna *is* the angel, so how comes she to be so bifurcated? Like that piece I read in TIME about the girl with two heads—Adrianna's like that. She lusts, I'm sure, but switches it to the other head and prays with this while that leers. What of the vagina they share? Does she play with herself, the lustful one, while the other keeps *that* vagina pure? She wanted my hands on her, why else was she tipped as far back as a far-sighted bifocaled fart until she was prone as Hells Angel on a Harley? Not me, old man, old child, old foetus, egg, weeping trembling for the new nude smell of her, desperate for interruption. And so it came, the snoop, snuffling nose, thank god for allergies among less privileged. Thank god—what anachronism, here in this school of deciduous drought, administrators trembling in prayer for new blood from beyond the waters. So we all suck. So we all wish to suck. Who was she? Not one of mine, surely. From nowhere. A devil? I must ask Anor, who sniffs everywhere, who will sniff for me, at me, if I demand it, he wants so badly to be taken under the professor's wing, arm-pit—malodorous, badly designed thing, particularly in a place where only computers are air-conditioned, the only valuable around, certainly not us. Panties even a bit ripped, to allow room for octopus to wave tentacle. Kill the microbe about to mutate, that's my job, always has been, it's called the status quo, beg her to smooth her little dress down over the black hole of her furry navel, or rise and loom above her to prevent heat from hastening mutation, not to select for an unknown, the only no-no, hereabouts. Except for quiet murder, that's always in fashion, ever appropriate, in the department of English.

Adrianna

The time comes for my punctuation. I easily see now why Jesus chose English for me—a battlefield of slashes, punctures, bullet holes, elisions, a veritable Catherine's Wheel of martyrdom.

All are going on all the time, of course, as I pray for those around me, all unknowing I do so to keep them alive in the Spirit. So heavy does mortality hang above me, like ! that I droop poor shoulders awaiting the slipping slab of it to fall on me, utterly obliterative.

Whispers to me: not for thee to know just when. Work thou musteth, in despite of distraction, among whom or which count Drs. Frank, Lloyd and Mr. Anor. Anor is a hook slanting down on me.

Pathetic this repetition of stage setting, which only delays my opening out to, bloodying myself on, impaling. Sacrifice = redemption.

But O I hear that infernal Anor sarcastic, shaking his sharp little familiar head: "What precisely do you sacrifice, earthling, why sacrifice, when your species actually enjoys the flesh bridge, temporary pathetic pontoon, dermous balloon of a moment, and makes of it a more than god's portion. Look, if you want to see what it's all about, do it with me, I'll show you a good time, it won't cost you a thing, and afterward you won't know it even happened."

"Accouch me with a devil! Fat chance, Anor. Harpooned by you I see myself dragged back to your familiar hell."

No, I sighed to myself, staring with something like sentiment at Dr. Lloyd's empty chair, imagining his weight on it even as he sometimes discreetly raises one buttock to allow escape to the inevitable results of beans, chilies and innumerable soft caffeinated drinks. May I but mention that flatus is near-allied to spirit; not for us to experience shock where it cares to make itself evident.

I will purchase and drag in a futon. If anybody asks me what for, I will murmur, "fatigue," the one disability taken seriously in this place, where god-sickness brings you only askance, alas.

As I do not pretend foreknowledge, I will not choose, the thing will transpire with the first person who enters my door and with whom I will lose that which I never strove to maintain: bodily virginity when what I crave is union with Jesus; but it is bruited about and whispered that to achieve it I must first unite with one like myself.

But what will be the fate of the one with whom I—?

I fear doom, a litmus between my teeth to locate the spirit, a buoy for the spirit no longer a boy, a reagent but never a prince. Therefore for this reason I actually hope for a stranger, as I maintain warmth for Lloyd and Frank and wish them no harm. Even if I were an ordinary hussy such a pairing on the floor were no good.

Secret-ary

They think it's easy as pie to sit here day after day a-smiling, wearing lipstick that's no more than crimson fire on my lips, sworn off kissing since I threw out that drunk no-good. I am a good Muslim woman follower of the Holy word of the Quran and I'd be happy as a mudhen in harim if Adrianna was to be in there with me, putting her cool face to my hot bosoms. Crying when she creeps back from off the brute's bed, I'd be right there in the dark to reach out and lick the tears from off those dusky cheeks, kissing cousin to my own complexion. I'd lick wherever she hurts, dear thing.

Damned world! Blessed Prophet, I'd ask you to take me away! to serve you head and toe in Paradise but my boy needs me, especially needs money and there's damned little I can scrape up plunked down here in the English Department. Now, in the Business Department, I done real well. Thank Allah I took that computer course. Helped me open a few files, produce some checks. The boy has such needs he used it all up, never had a chance to accumulate. Just as well, with adjustors swooping down like the damned Spanish Crusaders. Good thing by then the accounts was empty. Gambling. Whoring. I'd still rip out my damn husband's head of lying teeth give the boy one moment's peace. I would do that. I would do more, but he don't come around much since he told me about some business deal gone bad and I took a pistol to the one wronged him, whupped him good with it. He never knew I didn't have no bullets, wouldn't have known what to do with them if I had. I thought the boy would surely appreciate, but he didn't, just like his dad, stink of women and booze. I thought maybe I 'd try to get him and Adrianna together, but I don't even know if he's got a disease, my boy. It hurts my heart. I need to talk about it, but here in this damn place, all they talk about is tenure track, not the straight and narrow.

Chair

As I sit in my office at eight P.M., it is twelve noon in Llasa when all the bells and prayer wheels go off at once, raising such a joyous din every sort of bird—raven, humming, crow, vulture, owl—rises like a dark hand of many fingers and then, as though losing strength before the brutal cold sun, melts down upon itself and rams frozen fingers into every crack and crevice of the capital. No one keeps a secret from the probing hand made from god's questing birds.

Ojalá Potala! if only here too in the English Department, hand and fingers of god's feathered truth seeking out rot, decay, duplicity.

The others know to leave me alone every night at this time, even if they don't know why. I summon them, shaman of my dream-life, at their mid-day ecstasy, energy to spare, shoot some to me here in my state of seated intense breathless expectation, more comfortable now that Adrianna has gifted me with a lovely yin-yang pattern masquerading as a crude simple and cheap paisley futon—oh, she suspects, all right. I tremble to place my extended middle finger on the spot where her third eye trembles in twilight, figuratively speaking.

Trembling is in the nature of my universe, so I must needs dissemble. "It's Parkinsons," I whisper to Dr. Frank, knowing he will pound this "gold to airy thinness," spread it so that everybody has always known it. "Parkinsons," they whisper, "The Chair trembles with Parkinsons, will soon slow to statue-like immobility." So they do view me at meditation, but see only disease.

From mid-April, I begin at seven P.M. on account of day-light savings time, which arouses confusion.

But hear this: they are already here. Yes, they are, or *he* is. Which ones or one are or is he? Oh let that go, let's say what I really believe this, it will not be a committee, in the open or disguised, it will be someone of great familiarity who suddenly flings off his robe of invisibility or familiarity. It could be Anor Bulim, believing he descends from another planet, and so it is—Potala, Llasa, surely so far away as to be effectively another planet. Imagine inhaling ghee, clarified yak butter, or spreading it on Ritz crackers, it's funny. I tremble and laugh, movements that put the whole futon atremble.

But I am too human. I kneel on the futon. I put my nose between my legs on the futon, breathe deeply of Adrianna, where her ample bottom rested, her earth inches from the hairs in my nose which pass one from another into my skull and brain the message of Adrianna's teeming life as gathered from the massed odor of her sitting.

And from this manifestation of the world I come closer to becoming Dalai Lama, (Mongolian for "oceanic celibate") than from any other action or inaction I take on my behalf. Also Adrianna derives from Adriatic, surely enough of an ocean? It connects, as all the hairs in my nose connect world to brain to infinite.

But the schedule of classes for fall awaits my hand. I rise with Cindy's aid from the futon. She seems to understand that I await a sign. She is always inches away as I reach out a trembling hand or two. She does not flinch if I clench some part of her that is outstanding but not ordinarily available. She glows, I imagine because of a deep desire to serve engraved in her race, gender and faith, to submit, "Islam," her joy and pride.

Yet, something diabolic here, for her breasts burn under hand, there leaps from them the squeal of teeming rage, they are twin towers from which emit rays that may sear the very seats of civilization when and if she teaches herself her own power. For this reason, I withdraw my trembling hands as quickly as I possibly can, not wanting the English Department to be the agency by which Apocalypse is unleashed upon the world.

"Book sale," she whispers in my ear, impacting cilia cousins to hairs in my nose and twin bases to the apex which is my brain, and I grow dizzy with conflation of the feminine with female, the god-man suddenly demoted to man-in-god. In other words, I want to grab her, kiss those deeply wounded lips, which she renews a hundred times a day in front of a small mirror which reflects light from a myriad of fluorescent bulbs above her desk.

Heaving between her breasts like a mariner lost in a storm at sea, a small image of the Prophet, with whom in my mind I joined hands and prayed to the great goddess of all oceans: give us what we most desire. Let us lead or let us follow, but it must be clearly one or the other, not this ludicrous democratic confusion resulting in utter lack of movement. Let us not confuse passive with stony.

As if summoned, Adrianna entered with Dr. Frank to break the logjam. Lucky I had reclaimed my hands. No scandal. Another time I may plunge into the black unknown, perhaps never to re-emerge. So much worse the loss for humanity, but who knows, there may also be llamas there.

Dr. Frank

"I have been planning this for a long, long time," I announced to the assembled multitude—well, less than greatly multiple, actually only Cindy, Adrianna and Anor. They sat rather uneasily on the edges of their chairs, as though poised for prudent flight, small birds confronted with a mess of edibles that could rear up and bite.

"I do not bite. I am toothless as an old scone," paused, and as nobody laughed or even grunted, sighed, rather a hallmark with me, rubbed my paunch to disarm them—veritable jolly St. Nicholas, not Old Nick—Satan—which after all the purpose of this gathering is to ferret out.

"In our culture we tend to glorify that which may *ad lib* kill us, like NPR," I paused.

"National Public Radio?" Anor instantly murmured, to demonstrate his *au courant* status, forming in his astonished query a furrow like a kind of Ganges seen from ten miles up, running through his lofty Himalayan brow, cutting through the Valley of Indus, finally giving itself over to the Bay of Bengal, from whence issues God's own monsoon that drapes itself over the whole of India to slake its gargantuan thirst. "And also kills," I added.

"What does, Dr. Frank?" Cindy scoffed softly, used to my saying only a fraction of what is swiftly passing under my own, not so lovely, brow, more like an eroded stump of igneous rock, a feature of extinct volcanoes once awesome now only cutting to the wayfarer who traverses without adequate footwear.

"NPR, as mentioned heretofore. Exactly that. But does nobody here know what these initials really betoken?" not unlike one deposited into the slot that opens a gate onto the platform where like an entailed doomed virgin princess helplessly awaiting the behemoth to issue from its fissure to inhale her virtue whole we quizzically but casually glance up at the commotion starting somewhere near the corona of our sun.

"If it isn't National Public Radio, Dr. Frank, then is it television you wish to warn us about? Bad for children? Hell on wheels? Snafu?" Anor snorted smiling behind his hand, pretending to need to blow his nose. Cindy grimaced and got up quietly to fetch him a tissue, thinking, no doubt, about the vastly lower standards of hygiene practiced by Malaysians, which really hurt her, because most of them are fallow Muslims. She could understand desert dwellers—how *are* they to wash?—but to blow mucus from nares? Not necessary, anywhere. Adrianna kicked at Anor, who mouthed some expletive, pretended to have hurt his foot on the folding chair, covering himself. I wonder at their playfulness together, as well as Adrianna, so crammed to the top with unapproachable dignity otherwise.

"*Exactly* like SNAFU—short for Situation-Normal-All-Fouled-Up—a term invented by my own branch of service, the submarine, where jocular could become jugular in the beat of a heart, oh.

(Each of them more deadly than a trawler equipped with tons of depth charges as I silently run beneath attempting to foul their lines before they can fix my position.)

"I must continue to disappoint you all. NPR stands for Nitrogen, Periscope, Rapture."

"That's it?" Adrianna asked in her little but deadly voice.

"Perhaps Dr. Frank has something more hidden under his skull cap?" sneered Anor.

"Dr. Frank, I see you're a bit flushed, did that hussy accost you and leave out before we got here? I'll send an all-points bulletin—" Cindy announced, reaching for a phone.

"Give me five," I implored, slapping each of their hands, which rose to impact mine simply as a matter of defense. Smiling grimly, I went on: "I chose submarine service because I knew it to be the most dangerous of all services, most profound, most silent, that is, trapped under water I became a secular Trappist. Oh, I wanted the trapping, when the nitrogen level rose and even blank bulkheads twisted themselves into sardonic grimaces, I knew I was hallucinating, but we know now that even hallucination is a kind of reality, and I knew that the Demon, the Devil, the greatest of all consternations, lurked right behind the sheets of steel, was out there pressing on our frail frame, desiring to smash us flat the moment our collective nerve gave out. And that was always possible, because, I can tell you, it was at least as terrifying as to be here in this room with the three of you, and you know who you are, and whom you represent. Oh, no, don't begin to deny it with your clever games, I've been through too much to be taken in by that sort of thing. The funny thing is, I love each one of you, as possessed by that power that remained always on guard, never sleeping, less than three inches from my head.

"And I was full glad of it, mates, glad to know that the great Satan's hand and breath and mouth and teeth and forked tail swished closer to me than the head I was desperately in need of most of the time, for, my friends, when the ship began to shake, my bowels turned to jelly, to jello, at best to jerky, but that was actually constipation, another story."

"But it *sounds* so good, doesn't it, Dr. Frank?" Adrianna cooed.

"You can call me Gypsum, Little Friend," I allowed.

"How did you get—?" Cindy began, but I held her off.

"Another time, another story. I continue. As I mentioned, Satan sat on our ship, rode it really, astride like an infernal cowboy. We all felt it, only I was able to speak it right out. The rest of the crew sat at my feet of nights after reveille."

"Dr. Frank, Reveille is at—" began the Infernal Impostor. I cut him off.

"I know what it is, blockhead! Down there was always night, even if the clock said morning. It was night, I say, night of the soul, and the enlisted men made vigil with me—damned officers were too snooty, afraid for their status—silent vigil, pushing Satan back, back, through the waters, back to the shores of the Axis. Do you," I blared out, "actually think invasion ended the war? You fools, it was the power of our vigils did it, and would do it now, again, against you revenants if I only had my ship. But I am telling you, I'm telling you this," and my throat filled and my eyes gushed out, "I'm telling you this, because there is something here yet to save, and I won't let you eat it up, piecemeal, like rats from beyond."

"I assure you, Dr. Frank, Gypsum, as you prefer, that anything of the sort is far off the coast of truth. We have our green cards to think of, Adrianna and me, at the very least."

"You probably don't believe me, but just look at the schematic, see the periscope, 'an optical instrument for viewing objects that are above the level of direct sight,' what's that my friends, but—He Who lives above. And see this: what is a conning tower, but for raising the periscope another notch? Oh, the makers were not stupid, let me tell you, they were godly men like myself, but they had to work in silence, oblivion and prayerful hope. Just take a look at it!"

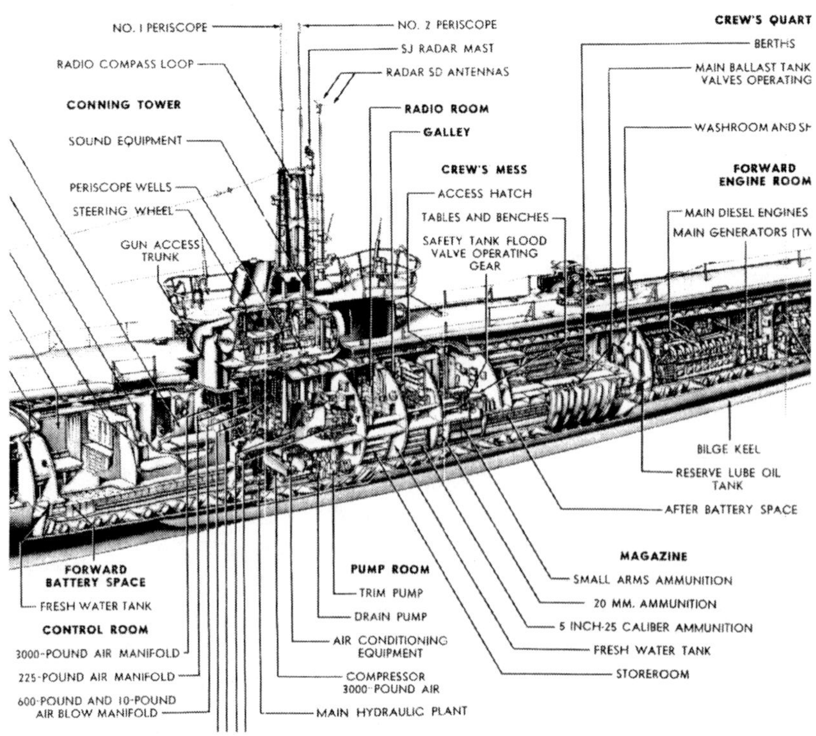

"Would it be too much to ask about—"

"I'm coming to it. Here it is: Nitrogen, Periscope, Rapture."

They all looked blank. Prelude to disappearance in a flash of sulphur, I bet myself. If words can do it, between Heaven and Hell, where I've positioned myself, these words will.

"When we were attacked, where neither periscope nor conning tower could come to our aid, when air became so foul we were like to die, we had to jettison ballast to rise free, that's where nitrogen and rapture came in. It was glorious—Rapture of the Deep, we all had it."

"Isn't that called 'The Bends?'" Cindy furrowed seriously, "It's supposed to be fatal, isn't it?"

"The Bends! Yes! All of us in an attitude of prayer, forced there by power infinitely greater than ourselves. Prayer. On knees, like this," I demonstrated, lowering myself craftily to a canister hidden behind my desk, invisible to all of them in front of it. All the windows and the door had been closed, sealed with toilet paper collected for months as I planned this moment. I threw open the valve. "There's no escape! I know nitrogen combines chemically with sulphur to produce nitric acid, sometimes nitroglycerin. Devils and demons are composed of none other but sulphur. Now let's just see if your master gets you out of this predicament without an explosion that will take us all at least part way toward the greater master of your nether realm."

I closed my eyes in prayer, hoping for at least a tiny fraction of a second of clarity before all my earthly tatters were blown to atoms.

Nothing. Opening my eyes a fraction, I saw, through lashes. Cindy. Filing her nails, not atomized. Adrianna, darkly eyeing Anor's suspicious new breasts, bent to help me up, sighing, "It was poorer in Malaysia, but fewer people were crazy, I believe. Will you turn that thing off, or at least crack open a window, it's very dizzy-making in here."

Cindy obediently threw open the windows. I kicked at the nitrogen tank, which hissed a little like an expiring snake.

Then they were filing out without a word.

"Wait! Just one minute more. Don't you want to know why they called me Gypsum?"

They did not tarry. They will want to hear in a more propitious time. Try again.

"Wait! Now I believe you are not demons, my friends. It was a test. You passed it. I'm glad. Now we can plan, plot, we can up periscope, man the conning tower, aid Dr. Lloyd to make this once again an English Department beyond compare. Wait, friends!"

They all tumbled like weeds through the outer office into the blank, uninhabited sunlight of the quad, where I watched them conferring at the flag, which by rights should always fly upside down in sorrow for the dearth of god on this campus.

Dr. Lloyd

I am of course ashamed, shamed. Shame is the ideal humble current to carry the message. I sit here in the corner, spider, as previously mentioned, waving one forepaw, or whatever spiders have they wave in the air, to catch the direction. There are airs from everywhere, airs on the G-string, airs from the orifices, little suspirations, operatic airs, ones I produce, and she has noticed it to my delight, from the elevation of a cheek, the gush of a tear from a gland, pushing emotion before it, it can be calibrated, but not yet, the wild chase of tear down downy cheek, slower if more decorated with irregularity, making no progress at all down a barbarous face like mine, where all the stoppage is in the Grand Canyon parted by the Himalaya of my nose. Shamed. Which is to pull aback, knowing too much, a Roertgen of a sonofagun. What makes it worse is that she is willing, all too willing for the sake of her lord, to make the sacrifice, to open her cave of winds to me, hoping that I will lose my way in there, starve, soon swoon, find myself before the shrine, before the holy of holies, that I will nerveless touch, having spent myself countless times before, finding my self raw and—yes—dripping, she doesn't mind the image or the thing itself, but where? O Lord, where will this abomination take place? Since she has no real private place except her skin in the chamber of her god, it must take place right here in this office, and I am meant to be vaulted above, with her. They are all mad, you know, mad, as I am sane. The Chair, who awaits his transmogrification—remember Adrianna wittily on transmigration—to Tibet, to dally with the llamas is his greatest desire, which he does not recognise as desire. Who knows, it could even be true, how should I know beside only being the container for that which is barely contained within him, he wants so to bless me, but doesn't dare, feeling that I am—yes, again, antechamber to his elevation. That's why he will even enter here, the mess I deliberately set, like a fire, and he also wants to be tied up in the middle of it, faggot for the feast of flame, rump to rump with noted Adrianna—not that he hasn't noticed what a fine storage of fat she carries in hers, fit for the fantods of flame as they start. Oh, yes, there is the Chair. And Adrianna, as mentioned, she is surely aglue with secretions from the bottom of the sea, mere maid now, goddess in the conch a latter day. Cindy in cinders, burnt up, also seeking immolation on ant heap, fearful only not all of the little formicidae-like myrmidons not be Muslim. She knows her immortal soul is toast, as she tastes in imagination the flesh of infidel Adrianna, desiring more than even Allah could imagine, concupiscent though he was, the feel of lip sucking nipple, like on like, current flowing back and forth, forth and back, gathering energy cyclonic, clonic in spasms of anus, puckering of sphincters, jolting energy from one station to the next, the whole rushing like a borealis through forever. Sucking's the ticket to hell for Cindy, but she does dare to carry it with her carefully hooding her eyes, but she opens them to me, for godsake I don't know why, stores some of it with me for godsake and I bloat O Lord, I am become a skin a water bag for another's desire, and I don't even particularly like her, as like a waterbug she'd suck me dry for sustenance, not desire, leaving me a mere ripple on the bottom with scum, nothing more than impediment making a little current producing a whisper of air for a motionless day, for the athlete winded from running as she believes toward the place where her god resides. Oh no, I am also married and she who patiently awaits must not receive a corpse on the current or discover it idling on the eddy unnoticed by any authority. But in her own way the Secret-ary seeks, howls in her wilderness of desk computer terminal printer and file, and I must listen or be blown over by the fury of her hurry. And what if Anor does come from another dispensation—who doesn't, pray? Don't you? Don't I? If belief can make it so, he makes it, so. He now has breasts, for godsake. I've felt them, jocularly. "How about those tits, Anor?" I shout jovially, for godsake, and took hold on them, with all ten. And they were really really there, even though the rest of him is a stick, like a mantis. Preternatural, "He's a preta-ghost!" might shriek Chair for the unnatural grown, two cancers perfectly spherical, appearing mid-semester. No more than imitation is greatest libation. Hoisting two breasts like beer in a size D cup, not even padded, miracle bras like Handel's Water Music for the Sovereign. Again water. I am surely meant to dissolve in rather than solve this conundrum, understand what is passing or to pass in the Department where I am willy-nilly the corner stone—stein, not cup. I expect Anor to settle soon on some part of me, not necessarily visible, to imitate and grow. What if it turns out to be mine fundament? Will he like it, shall I act as his instructor on the usufruct of it, since not a tool for every occasion, not hardly, only inconvenient, aleak with palpitation, circumscribed. Will she take it? Do we palm the disjoint twins together somewhere? No, no, we don't, it would be misunderstood by his mentor, Dr. Frank, who knows precisely where his Maker can be found, fathom five and counting, where passion and rapture ride together like hag on buck. Still, still, he has his secret, does Frank, his hands itch and sweat and twitch and fret, they do. He mages depth charge, torpedo propelling to its mate every time he takes a crap, praying for the sometime projectile ballistic, teeth-gnashingly disappointed by solitary turd. Down and down he goes, I see atmospheres piling one on the other like walls crushing in on him, eyeballs bulging, about to become projectiles themselves any second unless I can manage once again to disconnect him, by knuckling his ribs, chuckling his wattles. "Hey, Frank, zip your fly," he dutifully peers, finding the thing shipshape, ejaculates, "Avast yon Hebe," weakly whilom, and I've saved him again, for which he is rarely grateful, I presume to add. And that's all the time I have for Dramatis Personae, I've sleep to tuck in while I can, there's tomorrow, for now.

Adrianna

Futon! What is it for? Nobody passes outside my door anymore, it's as though I live in a time warp. I don't know where I am. Possibly I am going crazy. But that is surely not the will of the Lord. What is more likely is that the Demon has heard what I plan to do and is out to thwart me. How? How do I know that Anor has not already done what I plan to do? He can do it, he has the capability to do what I want to do, to become me, since he was already a long way along when he arrived here. Given the possibility he is only a fair-to-middling imitation of the Demon, still he has convinced me of his identity.

So, let us go on, logically reasoning together, seasoning our minds as it is integrity's sake in a college setting to do so. This is Department of English, all literature is on slow boil here, isn't it? So we forge ahead. Knowing I want to fling myself into the cauldron of sex, sacrifice, etc., whatever there is, Anor vexingly does it first. So it is me, after all, no real difference, neuron to neuron, entree, vegetable and dessert, none whatsoever. If Anor has sashayed into Dr. Lloyd's office, or Dr. Frank's or even opened herself to Cindy, it is as though I have done so in my own body, and will there be difference unto the Lord? Because I haven't been able to stop it, say, like Judith with Holofernes, how she did chop his gentile head while he slept, but I think he punctured her first, I believe so, but I haven't the Good Book by me here, it was stolen, along with Cindy's Quran, one night, by godless miscreants.

Ah, who can care? So long as below the heft of the hair in the hand swings the head of the monster who would cut short the hegemony— what's the matter with me? Everything like with an echo, "outside my door anymore," I am bad as Poe.

Steady, keep steady hand on myself. Look inside, see if anything is changed. For that I need a gynecologist, ha-ha. No, I don't, I can see—Adrianna, see!—it's what the Lord gave you, X-ray the interior, turn yourself inside out, put skeleton on exterior like crustacea, bony antennae to feel and smell what passes. Just do it, don't talk about it.

Still, one passes, I stir languorously on my futon, arch my abdomen toward the bank of fluorescent bulbs, the chaos of holes in the sound-proofing, moan inordinately trying to hook someone outside my petit cubicle, thrust my tiny precise pubic triangle toward Alpha Centauri and as hastily withdraw it—Anor may be from there for all I know and there may be more there like him if my "luck" holds true.

Which reminds me, I haven't prayed for any of them in a long time. Does this mean I am corrupt? Yes, it does certainly, and makes the sacrifice even more necessary and in the most immediate future.

There is a knock. I hear a knocking at my door. Someone is a-knocking. "Who is it? I'll be there in a minute." I must compose myself, settle my dress down around non-existent hips, no resistance there, O Lord. This is a dread moment. I snap on the lights, open the door, a crack.

Nobody, I know, someone however I would want to be, at least look like, in a tiny black dress, shining eyes boring into me, already undressing my corneas behind my tortoise shell glasses, utterly transparent to her, or to the demon disguised as a her.

"You might as well come in, but you're not one of my students, are you? Do you seek one of the senior staff? I'm only a long-term sub." I babbled, noting out of the corner of an eye that the futon like a toad's tongue had rolled itself out and lay on the wet chin of the floor.

A bewitching smile bubbled up from pearliest teeth, she groomed her shining blonde hair as it bosomed in an otherwise undetectable breeze—Venus being born before my eyes, not my kind of mythology at all, not my cup of tea either, I must step on her shell, nacreous whore under all that bloom.

But she did step in, over the threshold, carrying herself in her own arms, tenderly, as though incomplete twins, a single head on two bodies, one utterly a-throb, the other corrupt as hell squamous with worms and maggots.

"Yes," I replied to her unstated invitation, "I suppose we must lie down here together. Who takes the top? You see, I have no experience with this sort of thing, I cannot do the honors. I expect you plan to ingest me very much like your mother the mantis. Please, do not hurt me more than necessity requires. I long for sacrifice, but paradoxically do not wish to suffer a lot of pain. I'm just not prepared. Ant-hills, formic acid, but all at once, not sequentially, please."

Humiliating, to crave favors of the Demon, indeed! She/it might even be Anor playing games. I looked more closely, trying to separate beauty from the shimmer of light behind her emanating from the outer office. Was Cindy out there, and had she led this thing to me, all unknowing, Cindy?

Yes, I could detect a presence that appeared to be Cindy, but she was not moving, seemed frozen, like Job's wife—no, wasn't that Lot's wife? I was losing it, everything I knew, dissolved by the eyes of this chambered nautilus into whose corridors I was being led, softly and blindly, all the while lightly touched by the lacquered surface of her sliding walls, lured by the unearthly music inside her shell, into which all sounds of the world filtered to make new and mesmerizing music of the spheres, acting on me, dissolving me, perfume made of vinegar, salt and soda, this creature, of whom I believe Dr. Lloyd had indirectly spoken, relieved when unto him came Cindy to break the spell.

But who would break this spell on me? Also, I don't want it.

I lay myself on the futon, legs slightly apart, as flat as my cursed bottom hump might allow, but Paradise forfend! it was no longer there. When I turned terrified eyes on the apparition she smiled at me tenderly as a mother, apparently having tendered me almost my greatest wish. Yes, dense flesh had vacated the lower and taken residence in the upper, and she, smiling the smile of recognition, fastened her lips on the righter of my new breasts.

I don't care if God watches, I love her. I am hers and she is mine for as long as she keeps me top-heavy and topsy-turvy.

Anor

It's time I begin to doff disguise, I've been here long enough, I'm actually making no progress detectable to me, much less to my handlers in the other galaxy. But what galaxy is that? Am I shedding neurons the way Dr. Lloyd and The Chair are in their mad dash to non-entity, which is their kind of death? Here they are terrified of dying, but rush headlong toward it every moment, with every exchange of vital fluids.

And how they do desire to exchange those fluids! Their maker provided them with all the fluids they ever need, yet they eternally believe the other's are better, or something like that.

I haven't *got* it, I know, as Dr. Lloyd would say, taking my elbow (does he get his fluids that way?) perhaps he likes the knob there, perhaps it's the closest he can get to Adrianna, or my rival, whom I have yet to see, though I've detected her—she's an emissary from another dispensation, and I have to watch my back, although I'm so tired I don't even care if she wins.

Yes, listen in on my thoughts, Dominions, I don't care, read my lips, as they quaintly say here, as though something were imprinted on those dust catchers.

I do believe these creatures are more like the protozoa that barely preceded them, blind mouths, nothing more, so these lips they want to cement together are blind eating things. Do they kiss or do they eat, or do they eat what they kiss?

I looked it up. The closest thing is the Nudibranchia—when they meet blind on the bottom of the sea, they spread their mouth parts to engulf the other. But the other does it too. If they can't engulf, they kiss and then mate. And both are both, like me. I am like the Nudibranchia, but that was not the grand plan.

What was it? Why have they not told? Get them to rot, that was all. They were drunk, the Dominions, and so to send me here, what a joke. All right, very funny, I can be funny too.

You, Bosses, take a look in my mirror. See anything—shall I say different? You want to put Your lips around this baby, how about it? Just like that, here's another futon, a duplicate of the one just on the other side of this partition. I'm not going to claim any souls this way, but I'm going to have fun until You recall me, or until You tell me what the hell I'm supposed to be doing.

You had better watch it, I'm becoming more like them everyday, a little bit here a little bit there. I've given Adrianna something to think about, beside her god, and that's a certain something even more uplifting than that. Ha-ha.

That's it? Give some, take some away, confuse the whole issue. Is there a study being made? Are there assignments in any other quadrant?

Dr. Frank

One of the questions I ponder right now: which one will change least, Anor or Adrianna? Why, I may ask myself? Which one is acting on the other, or is there ever any way to ask that question so that it makes sense? In space, two bodies coming into contact and they each repel the other, cringe away, so if God and Satan meet in space, which one will be flung further into the empyrean, the cold, utter cold of outer hell—which?

But that would mean I am hedging my bets, attempting to predict which of the two great forces will triumph and thus throw in my lot with him (Lot—so good, thank you for throw-aways, Lord)

But as I look at them in my mind's eye, Anor with his new voluptuousness, there can be no question that we will ever hire him. But are they in league? The ploy should have worked, unmask them, but together, perhaps one vial wasn't enough to pierce their duplicate vileness in tandem.

I begin to see the sand settle as in the bottom of an hour glass, my isolation is meant to have an end, find a horizon for the orb, the sun to rise above, to testify my manhood unto God, to reproduce one of my own.

Not in the horrid way Adrianna and Anor have chosen to go, not like amoeba, not unnaturally. No, no, like a man. As I am a man, I react as a man, even in the untimely but forgiven blurts to Cindy, God love her for a Mussulwoman.

No. It will be the 3Ps—Posterity, Prodigy, Progeny. Forget Rapture of the Deep. Where this seed germinates is the deepest grimmest place of all—the womb!

Onto the hidden cracks and crevices of womanly sort, so like the very image of God's own fjords, their coastline an ever-ready surprise, harbor, blowhole, sandy beach, horrid rock to break the unwary, horrible squid in fatal embrace, liquified and sucked like strawberry soda, oh.

"Dr. Lloyd," came the timorous voice of that dark shining specimen of slavish always docile humanity.

"Yes," I replied, trying to maintain civility, because it was not her image I was conjuring, and I had guilt at it, she who had felt my hands on her person without repine, perhaps even hoping that, outside this vale of iniquity, she and I—it was not unknown even with such disparity in age, gender and race.

Yes, race. it must enter in. I cannot forget the Bible, though I know what bigots we must deal with in that day and age. If it were only one of the three, I could go for her, Cindy, Cinderella, Cinder-woman, but for the Progeny. I must think of progeny. It is time. Her child and mine could even be Prodigy, and Posterity might even thank me, but the Progeny itself, mixed, confused, spun about as in a genetic game of blind-man's bluff—not for now, no, no—thank you, not for my Progeny. So I must, I must say no.

"No. Cindy. I can't, although I would love to mix my blood with yours and I'm sure it's possible, there are entrances, precedents."

"*Dr.* Frank! Please stop that, we haven't been engaged in conversation before this minute. Keep up this outrageous behavior and I'll mention to the powers-that-be that you're in direct line for replacement by retirement." Her face fell, she looked mortified, her hand went to her mouth, her eyes grew round and leaked at the extremes. "There, I've said it, what others only whisper. Now if you want me to continue to protect you, stop that talk."

I kneeled and bunched up the cloth at her knees where it tended to wrinkle, kissing both knees—tasted a bit acrid, as though she had been puttering about in a mouse nest. "Thank you. Cindy. Best of friends here in the Department of English. I was only just thinking out loud, you know how I do."

She looked me up and down, calculating. "Never been married at all, Dr. Lloyd? And fixing to hitch up at your age?"

"May I rely on your discretion? Dearest Cindy? I am. It is true. There are the 3Ps to think about. No, no, don't start backing away, there will be no more explosions, not a single one. Look, no nitrogen. Nothing like that. Come back."

I trailed behind her into the outside office where she cowered sobbing disconsolately behind a steel file cabinet. I followed her around, we played ring-around-the-file-cabinet. All at once she stopped, put herself in an attitude of Islam, and appeared to wait for the end.

"There, you see, truly I'm safe. Yes, I want to marry, I want to produce children, at least one, to carry on my work. And I must admit, I thought of asking Adrianna for her hand."

Cindy flushed darkly. "Adrianna! If I'd known she put out her hanky for you—"

"No, no, no hanky-panky, she knows nothing of this, nothing. But look what I can do for her, the Green Card above all, medical insurance, a strong man to defend her against marauders."

"But Dr. Frank, you're not a strong man, not young, you know it yourself, never have been as long I've been here. You do lists, and that's all. And what is this about prodigy—?

"Posterity. Prodigy. Progeny. But I must be careful. There are two meanings to Prodigy. The prodigious, like Samson, not likely. The prodigy like Einstein, also regretfully out of the question. And there are other prodigies like those in the heavens, like two-headed girls— do you remember the article in LIFE—?

"You showed it to me already. You had me duplicate it. You made a bad joke."

"My fault entirely," I apologized humbly, "but," I continued with excitement, "who can tell if this is a gift from God or a punishment. How can we ever know? Every decision is desecration and sacrament. But I can tell you who does know."

"Who, Dr. Frank? Cindy murmured, leaning wearily against the file, in peril of over-tipping it, so I hurried to shore it up on the other side. Thus we found ourselves, chins on the top, like figureheads on galleons, speaking across frozen gun-metal.

"Why, the very person with whom I intend to press my suit."

"I don't believe there's a Chinaman's chance Adrianna knows how to press your suit, Dr. Frank, and why would you ask her to?"

"Never mind. The point is, I don't know if Adrianna is sent to me from God or Devil, but it is none of my business. I'm not sure it's even any of her business. That she is pure—pure good or pure evil— of that I am sure."

Cindy's face hardened, she sniffed loudly. "If you're going to take up with Adrianna, I want to be sure your intentions are honorable. She's got herself a futon in her office cubicle set off from Dr. Lloyd. I don't know what she's got planned for that bed, but I don't like it one little bit. I don't like the look on her face. I don't hold with arti- ficial implants like she suddenly showed up with. Do you know what those things cost, Dr. Frank?"

"Those things? Ah, I believe the surgeon lopped them off the back and sewed them on in front, didn't he? So she probably got them cheaper, since he mined the metal on her own land, so to speak, right?"

Cindy aimed at me a look of complete scorn. "You don't know

anything at all, Dr. Frank," her eyes commencing to leak again, "after I've looked after you all this time, off to the first pair of plastic tits you lay your eyes on. Men are all the same. My boy ditto. Where's honor, real honor?"

"Cindy." I said, trying another tack, "How would you handle yourself with a two-headed daughter?"

Cindy withdrew so suddenly from the file, it overbalanced, tipped and fell, myself on top of it, as though trying to embrace it in some ludicrous way. Cindy didn't even look.

"You're a racist, like the rest of them."

"But Cindy." I yelled at her as she went through the door, toward the women's room, I was sure, where I couldn't follow her, "Adrianna's black like you."

"She's Asian, you ass," Cindy hissed over her shoulder.

I stopped, stunned. Connections! Asian! Could she be, with Anor, the committee the Chair always expected to carry him off to the Palace of Potala? Could they be unconcerned with me, but only spying out the lie of the land with Chair? My heart sank. Was there to be no 3Ps for me?

Not possible, I told myself, carefully disconnecting myself from the overturned file. Whose? Never mind, still, there were lacy bits of paper sticking out of various drawers. The residue of strong female perfume permeated the air. I looked around. Cindy gone, nobody. Was this truly a college or some place ordered out of time and space? Never mind that either. Someone was huffing and puffing up the stairs. I grabbed the nearest, fattest file that smelled the strongest and ran into my office just in time to avoid whoever it was.

Chair

Atremble, I tell myself that this is what I want, systematic divestiture, progressive impoverishment, until I am so close to being a wraith the Committee can snuff me into their nostrils and never even have to declare me on their manifests as they fly onward to the Navel.

Do they tell me this? Do they tell me anything? The point is this: my history has been spirited out. Oh, I don't mean to demean the word "spirit," it's not spirit, it's my past here, my entire past, gone, stolen, or at least gone. Every perfumed letter, every syllable, every carefully parsed irony. I admit it, they were my students, I resisted circling errors of agreement, tense. The agreements were tense, how could they have been otherwise—little motels charging equally paltry amounts, paid for in cash, accrued slowly from, Oh God! book sales overseen by Cindy, small amounts purloined from her accounting—did she know? Does she know? Does she keep a list somewhere? I never thought—does she have a duplicate key to everything, and has she read all those letters? Damn it, Cindy, this is all I have, at least until I can transubstantiate pants into robes, grays for saffrons, and a begging bowl.

To become clean. I feel Adrianna pining toward the cleanliness of being chewed by ants, on antheaps, but I will cleanse my lust in the light of humility, begging at the entrance flaps of the poorest of the poor. I will get to holiness before her.

Before her entrance flap, what! an image, I am myself as ever, never change. She lies separated from me by her little flapping material, on her futon, immobile, unspeaking, as I tug at her buttons—in my mind. I occupy the biggest office, windows on two sides, why was I so stupid as to put her in with Dr. Lloyd, who does not deserve her, being married, with progeny. What put that word in my mind? I never use that word. Never mind, mere splinters separate us, splinters however driving deep into my brain, separating me as though in a cage from the Holiness Police.

If Cindy has them, I am safe, she will but weep for the sullying of purity over and over again. Virginity in every generation of students streaked by my gummy paw. It isn't as though, however, I wasn't sought out, they did so, every one of them, I never took the long first step. They hiked their jammies, yawned and snuggled in before I fell in love with them. I didn't resist, why should I? once I ascertained their sincerity. I hurt no one, these were sweet secrets, nothing worse. I helped them, an application here, recommendation there, but that's not why it happened. We were mutual stepping stones, confirmation of thrust of mind and body, dress rehearsal for her, passive but enfolding carbuncularity on mine. She never expected gymnastics, I demonstrated chiefly indelible gratitude. We never passed glances in class, if she still danced attendance, all transpired customarily postgrad, there was only courtship while I could still pen "A" for adultery in her record. I say "she," I say "her," but there were many over the years, yea, how many? Cindy would know. Cindy knows. She has stolen the records—for what purpose? Blackmail? Only deep embarrassment is possible, not acts criminal. So I believe. So I think. Well, I don't know what's in there except repetitious intimacy, unique sexual jokes original and repeated by different people, pictures of her in her youth, as though her age at the time here wasn't young enough, photos of her dog, still young enough to have that primary relationship with Dog, Mom and Dad—who were my age at the beginning, much younger than I as years accumulated, until even parents could be my children, and the she I played with—what, my grandchild? Do I remain here, an ancient horror, flapping on my own clothes line, so out of phase with my consorts nothing makes slightest sense? But is that what is required, that everything be reduced to dust and ache, before my transport arrives to take me away from the Department of English?

Secret-ary

Gall, bitter gall, I want to throw up, I want to expel it all, right in their whited sepulchres like I was raised to do. It has to come out, I'm still the Baptist chile with round round eyes pushed off my Daddy's lap and forced to trot down in front of the congregation to be saved, baptised in the Blood of the Lamb, evil-smelling water everybody and his sister has already been in with God knows what germs, but terrified as I was I survived it, though I believe I was being drowned from some crime I couldn't even imagine, held under so long, I do believe that preacher didn't take aholt of my crotch by accident. Nobody ever taken aholt of my crotch by accident, it has always been by design, and not God's, not by a long shot.

Still, I retain love in my heart, I don't know how, since I been at the receiving end of betrayal so often by nearest and dearest, sweet-talking, bitter-acting. Gall, it galls me. I knew a tree surgeon, white—ever know a black tree surgeon, easier to climb a tree. He explained to me why a tree grows one of them things, like a tumor but on the outside, big, round thing, doesn't seem to bother the tree. He told me it was a place the tree grew to store the lies people told each other as they passed by, year after year. Oh, I knew even then it was just a story for a little girl to hear, and he didn't really care about me, but in some way it's probably true, it probably is a place where a lot of poison is stored up to keep it from the heart and lungs of the tree. Keep it boxed up below in one place so the rest of the tree can reach up to

God. Like tubercules trapped, as long as there's strength and little white soldiers in there to keep the TB trapped. Lose strength, defenses break down. I don't know how much longer I can keep it up.

Because they're on me. Look at that Dr. Frank, poor soul, I guess he kind of forgot he's already married—how much more out of it can you be? Wants little Adrianna, betwitched, bothered, bewildered, bedeviled, likely. Wearing falsies, hoping to catch a Green Card, catch a swan out of here to meet her god there on a pond. Only God out there is swatched with slime, I've seen that. I could take her home with me, once she's clobbered, nurse her back to health in my house, save her from these hyenas laughing and squeaking like bats putting their dirt all over her. All they produce is dirt, they call it syllabi, but it's really only the dripping tongue they speak in, like when I was little and grown-ups so earnest spoke in ancient real tongues, I was so little spit rained down on me 'til my nappy hair was all wet and scummy. I hated it, right from the start, that's when my change-over to Islam begin. I was so glad—no more baptism, no more hot manhandling with rough skin and tearing nails. Respect, respect.

Why do I kid myself? What respect? Just more work, grease, sweat, slavery to the man. Shut of the men, I can pet Adrianna when she comes to me, trembling, invaded. I can help her kill the soldier, we can kill them together, with our lips, we can groom each other, kill the fleas, I'll fill up my system with them if necessary, I can suck the evil spirit out of her I don't care where it's lodged. God of Jehovah spits me out, Islam allows, thank God.

She asks me, "to prepare for intimacy, Cindy, how is it best? I don't want to appear foolish or suddenly disappear. I have heard of a thing, 'dildo,' what is it?"

I don't know where to look, I'm not saying I haven't used one when things and the going got tough, it's not as though they're made of pork, Alla has nothing against them from what I read in the Quran.

"I know it is my destiny and desire to be united to the next man who solicits me, I must submit. Your religion is a life study in submission, Cindy, you must instruct me."

I thought, "So this is what Dr. Lloyd has been getting at with his ant-hills, his St. Catherine's wheel, how he looks at her, the astonishment and gratitude in his eyes when he saw her coming rather than going with her new additions. Men don't care what's real, his rapture was real even if the tits aren't." But I don't even know that with the weirdness going on around her since Adrianna and Anor arrived almost at once, almost as one.

She's in there, waiting. Or maybe not. She's hasn't talked about it for awhile. She doesn't seem to be waiting anymore. Maybe one of them has done it to her, maybe she's off bleeding somewhere by herself?

That hussy in the black dress, has she been in there with her? Is that enough for her, to lay with a ghost?

I bought the thing, it's in a neutral package, about a foot long. It would go neatly between us. I could catch her if she fell.

I went back to see if Dr. Frank was alive or dead. The Chair's file was out and all over the floor, Dr. Frank's door was closed, lights off, but I know he's in there, probably sniffing nitrogen or some such. I must rescue Adrianna before she truly kills herself.

Dr. Lloyd

All the mailboxes stuffed to the gills. If they were fish they'd be dying of oxygen deprivation. For that matter, everything is stuffed around here, why to the gills? Every skin like a police cordon, strained by the rage of what's trying to get to the other side of the line. Everything wants to break out, everything swollen, even the eyes of the creatures, glaucous as three-days-dead mice, black inside, giving out no clue of the specific kind of horror while dying. Everything is either dead or dying around here, no hope. To look at the material, you'd think there was nothing but life and gaiety, but no, it's sneak and snuff. Why oh why didn't he just take them out, sashay around with them on his arm, saying: "This here is my concurrent chatelaine, not bad for an old honky, eh, you'd never know her father's a stevedor and the mother takes in laundry." He's the one could do it, he ought to be able to look beneath a surface, he sure wants the llama-police to do it with him, or is he like so many other hypocrites? Who could have hated him so much as to do this thing? Unless he did it himself, to proclaim independence from the society of his former fellows. Why not, and it's kind of advertising as well. Still, the Dalai Lama must be celibate. I'm sure Chair has always wanted to be celibate but lacked the balls. Amazing how style never changes, evolutions hieratic, like Egypt. No doubt Chair as Pharaoh in a great rush once the initial puncture took place got it over with with dispatch, accouched and soon delivered her wrapped nicely to someone of her proximate generation. Doubtless he attains a certain immortality in this way, surely he learned to fake ejaculation—how were they to cotton to it, barely out of pinafore? Thus saving precious rare drops for God on the throne in the faraway palace. Even

Adrianna is attracted, but probably for very practical reasons. Anor will lie and die with Chair before she will, I ween. And what makes me so superior to all those? At least they know their stump and keenly miss the limb. I however sit here immobile, all limbs struck off, a mere hologram of a man, pretence, sham. I could snatch the fragrant poison from out each box, while imagining the box of each of the fragrant poisoners, save him. Does he want saving? I interfering busy-body, den-father? Surely, he doesn't want to be laughing-stock just yet? I shudder to think what Secret-ary might do with this. Why hasn't she seen to it before? She is glued to the door of my office, waving her hand slowly back and forth. If the place weren't already so weird, it would make a funny picture, but we are used to even more here, now. I wonder when her appendages change place or shape. If I begin to remove them, will she ask me what I'm doing, and insist on watching? She is in a kind of swoon, but I'm sure something like that would be certain to revive her. I have no choice, since evening classes are about to begin and some one of the hourlies will surely arrive to check her box any minute. Authority must be maintained, beyond the person. Chair holds the Chair, occupies the Chair, continues the Chair. He is in practice for the Chair. Therefore, I must do it. Perhaps I can send Cindy on a journey. "Cindy, I realize you are doing something absolutely vital maintaining vigil in front of my office, but I really must open the door. May I ask you to go the student store to get a copy for me of the latest book of Alexandrine Couplets?" For answer, she peered sharply into the shadows of my office, where I often leave the light off, hoping I will discover Adrianna or the Other in an inky corner. So I am a possible suspect. Of what? That Adrianna has been here is without doubt, as the futon shows unmistakable signs of activity, its rubbery surface only now coming back to its initial shape. In fact, a quite strong activity, leading to minute abrasions and even cuts in the central fut. Cindy still hanging on the door, a vacant look occupying her face, shell-shocked, Dr. Frank might opine. "Go get the book!" I said sharply, simultaneously slapping her. How dare I? Her eyes opened. Something in her responded with outrage. Suddenly, I kissed her. That broke it, she slumped against me, hanging on to my neck, sobbing. "That little darling, eaten alive!" "What little darling, what ate her alive?" Alarmed, I knew. The same apparition that had come unto me, we all wanted her (it), the Department was haunted. But I didn't have time. "Lie down there, Cindy, you need the rest, I'll close the door." Suiting action to word, I ran out, blocking the door with a curiously upended file. I stuffed handfuls of papers into a wastebasket, frantically looking toward the outer door as I did it. After all, it is a Federal crime to touch a mailbox without authorization. But maybe not in the English office, still I didn't want to take a chance. It was more than time for people to begin filing in, followers of the great god Ra. Words ran off my fingers down my arms as I clutched the filmy missives, "care, love, longing, tease, hair, nails, shower," I was awash in the echoing mirrors of homogeneity, all flat two-dimensional, no sense of desire, vertigo, pain, death—nothing real, only perfume and calculation. A mathematic universe, and then I realized something else—Chair hopes for the utterly linear, chair with four exactly placed legs, the genetic even Mendelian formula that puts him at its apex, inevitable. The chaos that we represent here is greatest agony to him, the music of the spheres repeats, contains a coda, is always sonata allegro. God for him is no more than a vertical pipe, an elevator of many floors, all exactly separated one from another, and he wills himself placed in the vortex, passive, given over. What a crock. I'll break it. These papers are an attempt to provide him with an updraft, but they will not be found. I will destroy them without burning, and he will be back to ground zero. Let's see what he does then.

Adrianna

It proves my point, everything in this culture depends on breasts. I've never so much as received a drop of mail in my box before; now my box runneth over, I am troubled only by the apparent fact that my admirers are all female. Or female demons, also possible, considering the visitation I have undergone—or not—but perhaps it was a dream on the floor in Dr. Lloyd's office—who can calculate the generations of feet that have left their indelible desires on it, neither is it cleansed at timely intervals. Who knows how we receive what we do receive, and for what we do receive, O Lord, thank You, in Your indecipherable darkness, in which I am locked.

Well now, here I am in the outside office, a little curious why Cindy isn't in her regular place, wondering a little bit why a file is shoved up against Dr. Lloyd's door. But who am I to be curious about all the odd ways of the Department of English? I'd better get used to them if I want to be one of them after this propitiatory semester.

"Onliest, when will you tell her, oh, not when, how, or do you want me to? I can face her. You have made me strong . . ."

Who does she want me to tell? Cindy? Has one of my students, there is no name given here, glimpsed by chance what passed between Cindy and me? It was after all strictly a pedagogical session, we didn't even see much of each other's bodies. Cindy's inherent modesty forbade, and I am of another faith. Fortunately, what bonded us was neutral, even the hue of it, neither this nor that.

Another, naked, but so young, what a charming little thing. She was *so* young, why does she want me to see that? Does she desire to produce another like herself? In this dispensation, O Lord, I am at Your service. I may reproduce, but surely this requires a male? Same child? half in shade, shadow, half in light, perhaps at the seashore, blurry vague images of what? Daddy and Mommy? A sib, or perhaps a little swain pining his tiny heart out at the little girl in her bathing frock who is dimpling pitilessly at another little boy.

"You promised me that, if we worked out, you would acknowledge me facing the world naked together instead of naked in private only *en face*, effectively hiding our genitals—we might as well be girls together."

Surely a French major, even demonstrating a certain Gallic *insouciance*, but the meaning of that word is "light-hearted unconcern," and this letter is anything but. Does she mean to do me injury who has never spoken to her?

No. Lord! I can see now how stupid I am, how ego-maniacal to believe these letters were actually meant for me. Bitter, but a relief too. To whom *are* they addressed? No address, no name, just letter after distressed letter, what an amount of fluid hyper-enriched blood courses through the fingers of these hand-penned missives, truly missive, because they fly of their own between the panting breasts of the women, really girls, to the probable man as their target. And what a cruel man to allow this sort of thing to happen again and again, and I certainly don't see many differences among them.

Let us then attempt to apply severe English heuristics to these documents. We see the thesis is ever the same: despite differences between us of rank, age and serial number, we are destined to sally forth openly into the world as a couple. The arguments are not obscure, they relate mainly to body fluids, but why are body fluids so important?

Sweat, semen, vaginal secretions—normal parts of the body day, only they churn out in increased volume with sexual excitement, but every one, even I have them I own, particularly when I think of Jesus, yes, You, Lord, I'm not ashamed. You gave me the wherewithal to praise—in nature every stream, lake, rivulet and trickle attest to the power of the Lord—and so I do.

No conclusions offer themselves up at this time; therefore, I must scurry to find a secure place to secrete these documents for now. The owner of them ultimately will break cover and approach streaming with anxiety to reclaim them. A simple yet non-judgmental modus allowing that to happen will come on me.

I'm not sure that, like these sweating girls, I have in fact entered the physical world by the renting of my hymen, because, strictly speaking, I have not been jointed by a man but only with a thing, if indeed it is possible to separate so cleanly man and thing.

Also I do not know to whom or what I owe my new prominence in the Department. I suspect Anor, but only because I suspect him of and for all mischief. As noted, however, we appeared here at the same time. My suspicions are aroused, alarm bells ring in my breast. I even perceive dimly both of us as one hurtling head over heels through thin space from—where? Heaven? Hell? From one and the other, exploding in duplicity somewhere out there beyond the reach of earthly telescope or science?

Is this a joke, God?

Anor

Atmosphere charged, lightning flashes in every corner invisible to all but me, nonetheless there. Adrianna's grim face from every facet, jutting chin, just perceptible horns from above or cleverly teased human hair, cheeks with peach fuzz struggling out of smooth skin, nose aimed like a knife driving forward with lips just behind to snatch up and rend in pieces.

I shudder, not entirely Adrianna-proof, particularly since she scents the truth, and it makes her furious. The whole idea was to get her pissed at the Department, see what kind of chaos she could wreak with hypocrites and idealists, fundamentalists and mystagogues.

An idle afternoon in Heaven and Hell, discussion of the nature of marriage as against elective affinities: The Prince of Dominions scoffs at the Lord's ideas about Moses—all DNA in place, The Prince holds Moses had no choice, no, not any more than did Job. God trembles with anger, but while creation teeters on the edge of dissolution, the Devil's logic holds fast—logic is more eternal than even The Old Fart.

I could hold her off a minute or so with my insubordination—blasphemy she would endearingly call it. I could hold her off a minute more by calling up The Adored One, but how clean the rugs after? I'm sure of one thing, I've got to keep her alive until we're picked up, sent back, because if there's a slip-up, producing even one more martyr, the whole thing could tip in some way, I don't know how, but bad news for us.

Surprised? That I'm so more specific than before? Well, things are more dangerous, closer to a boil, closer to busting open, to releasing a multiplicity of sportive cells, cancer, they call it here, what I need to remember to check every night within to prevent their crafty incursion into my oh-so-human constituents, sublunary as presently presented.

The moment she lies with me, we become one, proving God's marriage contract. If we only look longingly at one another, we are the picture of lust, Devil's compact. I can offer her money, but she won't take it. How about a job? Snatch the tenure-track job myself and then humbly offer it to Adrianna? Probably not actually possible. Turn her into Marilyn Monroe? She probably doesn't even know the name! Take too long to get her to long for it.

She has to fall for me. Pity. Pity, right, pity is probably the royal way. "It won't cost you anything, Adrianna, but I am growing even thinner over the painful thought of you, out there, in danger, when I could enfold you in my wing—" strike that, image of bat, I'll bet. "—wrap you to my bosom,—" not either, she's suspicious particularly of her good lumps—does she feel fluid coursing through them? Should I provide her with the means to gravida? Convince her that the super-expensive model dildo she and Cindy shared was really studded with sperm, freeze-dried, taken from genius, no refrigeration required? Possible. Possible. But would she want that? After all, her built-in desire is to self-destruct, or at least find an agency who can do to and for her. Suppose I offer that? A blade slipped between her ribs? Is it all right to do it here, or must it happen in a much more public place, like do I hire a team of wild horses to tear her apart in a stadium, between innings?

I admit to love-sickness, Dominions. Is it because she is part of me and I of her, that I gravitate to her, hoof to head, hair to hide, and pine to think what she thinks, feel what she feels, yearn what she yearns? I have ceased to be, and I am no longer her, in this place here am I male, whatever that may come to mean, as she is female, which she explores ever more actively, but for my part I no longer consent to be the agency for her to shed body fluids, now precious to me because they flow in her.

Hear all that? I am subordinate, I'm sure just as planned, You Two. If They only knew how Their surmises have turned out curiously correct—Plato told Them, didn't he, but They didn't listen closely? Philosophers were closer to us in the old days, eh, Boys?

Selective infinities, that's where I'm at these days. Equipped with Dr. Lloyd's penis acting like a pendulum as it climbs to east, then to west, blind wet foetus-maker, pathetic, but here they all are, yet cells know where to go, patriotic little soldiers for god and country, aren't they? Then, how did mine get to their places? Nothing arbitrary, all remotely operated for every generation. I must study this more closely, Adrianna may pose questions.

They'll all get what they deserve, regardless of directive. I haven't even checked my box for days. I must stay out of the way of lightning bolts, which can pierce even me, armored as I have made myself since the inadvertent near-miss of the early days of Adrianna's accidental power.

Pity, yes, on her part, need, desire, yearning on mine. Adrianna, how beauteous thou art, how like mine own heart's desiring.

Oh, but I disgust, don't I? Put mentality into a body, clamp on a pecker, and it goes roostering and rooting in all erections, how little free willy-nilly.

I could request use of a submarine, whisk them all aboard, in the process probably killing old Frank with joy and the Bends. Or I might host a conference in Llasa with Chair as chair, rendering him speechless. Make Cindy's boy king of Morocco with complete power over her, to her infinite delectation.

But Lloyd, Dr. Lloyd, who knew me from the git-go. The only one thinking of anybody but himself, and why? What if I got his wife to rise and shine, get up and shout. She sits silent, sunk in herself, year after mute year, cleaned and re-set by minions, like a human termite queen, huge, dense. He stands by her, never speaking an ill word. I am instructed? I am not. I am afraid going to that place.

But the illusory one is not, the one who comes and vanishes, as though she took her complete cue from Botticelli and the conch,

appears to all but me, giving rise in me to a suspicion that she is a branch, a spur track, of me, testing them all. Did I ever boast I knew the whole mission? Pretend?

I'll wait for the lush perfection to present herself. What else can I do but wait?

More like Adrianna than not, after all, I wait on Your Will.

Dr. Frank

I am become a burr under my own saddle, a mockery, outcast from everything in which I profess to believe. How could I have done it? First to take them, second to distribute them. Did Brutus have the right? Was Mata Hari punctured for the good of nations? Quisling to preserve his northern kin from southern barbarians?

I reserve the last and most grating for a new paragraph: Judas. Do I believe, under my former cloak of piety, the Chair grows too large a seat for comfort? For equity? For the Department I have called home for long ages? I who desire to close the circle, dynastically speaking, by taking Adrianna home with me.

Another dastardly thought not to become deed. I am married. I own it. I applied for conference funds, Cindy reminds me. What would I do without Cindy? I may have to, if I go further and further into the pit, down where there can be no light, beyond reach of help, of air of—even—God.

Judas believed in his right too, his right, too. Jesus must be stopped. Why? Because he was shredding the fabric of the Department, so-to-speak, breaking in a new dispensation unknown to any of them, some were quite willing to try it out, but not Judas, eternal conservative, who instead cracked the skein of the Fisherman of Souls.

What of Adrianna? When she finds I have betrayed the Lord, she will not hesitate to slaughter me. I will not be safe in my bed, and she knows where I live, and even if she doesn't, she can consult her infernal partner, who will fly her to my side, the one with my heart in it.

What if I sleep on it? Then she can't slip the knife, perhaps. Never mind, she is not so literal, they are not so careful where she comes from.

It was secretly thus: fighting the devil in the persons of those other than U. S. nationality, I became intimate with him, I knew him millimeters from my ear, always furious and ready to stab with his sharp tongue through my head in one ear and out the other, but he never could manage, solid maintenance of the sub kept him out, until now. Then came Adrianna, Devil disguised in piquant costume, as he can do, having no care for gender distinctions, and I thought, for my final act, I would fling myself on her, catch the Devil unaware, and kill him forever.

No more silly juvenile attempts like nitrogen and the rest, no more poking myself where I don't have staying power to stab—what an idea anyway to graft my genes on to those of the Demon—did I, could I, actually believe they would persist and conquer those eternal damned ones?

How did I ever become so arrogant? We know, arrogance is a mask for a quivering behind, simpering anus, vacancy disguised as occupancy. Where did I leave my wife behind? Do we in fact live together? I must solicit Cindy, but where is she?

I must remember all I have perpetrated by the word JAB: for Judas, Arnold, Brutus. I will importune the Chair for forgiveness. It is perhaps time for me to depart this vale of fears, this stale bunch of steers mooning over new comers, fresh blood who don't even circulate blood.

Perhaps it was all jealousy, as I saw them enter his office, first hesitant, then confident—they were inspirited; while I sat and brooded on God, he gave them of himself. I was Dead Sea to his Galilee.

So it was no good on the bottom of the sea, it is no good here on shore, I am castaway, rags decayed in my moral obloquy, a whitened sepulchre—actually, the term was a gift from Cindy.

Now I must do it, rip these rags from my rotten frame, and crouch on the floor, inviting all to spit upon me.

"Dr. Frank, stop that, you're making a spectacle of yourself. Oh, dear, has it come to this? Time for the men in white suits. Help!"

There she was, on cue, Cindy, my own Cindy, but she cannot make me go back. Still, her efficient fingers so like a mother's force back on my shoddy underwear, my stained pants, she stuffs in my shirt, her long fingernails unwary cruel cutting deep furrows into my soft pallid unhealthy skin, she stands me in the corner, licks her hands and smooths back my sparse hair.

"There. Take your clothes off again, and you're meat for an institution—that's baloney to you, Dr. Frank. Why did you do that? You've never done that before. Leave you alone for a minute—"

"My dear Cindy, I am become anathema."

"You never had asthma before, Dr. Frank, why are you having it now?"

"It is time for me to be gathered into the bosom of my ancestors, Cindy."

"Even at a time like this you cannot even for a moment stop thinking of bosoms. I declare, once a man, always a boy."

I couldn't see clearly for the moisture in my eyes, I put out my arms blindly for her, but she kept carefully out of reach. "Even you reject me, as I deserve. I thought I acted in the best interests of the Department, making public what Chair has perpetrated over years with one after another innocent student."

"Oh, you mean those letters," Cindy sniffed, "big deal, you all do it, he's just a documentation freak. You're all disgusting, every last man jack of you, including the ex and my degenerate boy. I'd cut off everything you hold dear if I only had the chance, and that's a fact, if you want to know, since you've apparently gone round the bend for the last time. You had to know sooner or later, Dr. Frank, and I thought because you were from the Under Sea Service you knew better than most how to contain yourself, since that was what you did, according to you, for most of your life. I thought you had some little ability to hold back, hold off, hold in. Hell, was I ever wrong."

Distracted, I fondled one of my buttons.

"No, you don't, Dr. Frank, touch one of them or your zipper, and I'll floor you with this 3M tape holder."

"3Ms? What do they stand for? Never mind, I don't intend to disrobe again. Cindy. Promise. It was a momentary aberration. I now believe I still have an important role to perform. By disseminating the purloined letters, I have perhaps provided acid sufficient to dissolve the false surfaces here in the Department of English, as well as to flush out those who are hiding in the interstices, thus to bring to speedy resolution the intolerable tension under which we have so long suffered."

"Does that mean you might start teaching some classes, Dr. Frank?"

I ignored the obvious sarcasm and replied, "I do not mean that. Cindy. I mean something much more important. There are consequences of galactic scope afoot here. What they are you will in due time be informed."

Chair

Finally, there is legacy, a bequest from the past or ancestor, also in the sending forth of legation, and even the legato, smooth, successive connected tones—all these in one, a sort of trinity, that which I leave the Department, as I do leave, as I spin off, not caring to wait any more for them whom I no longer feel clean enough to name.

Clearly loss does not always result in minus value. They all left me so long ago I never knew that all this ugliness was desire, vain desire, to replace them—wife, child, animals, dead and gone, taken so young their moisture's perfume had no time to dry—wet behind ears and everywhere else.

It was innocent, all I wanted was to frolic, I desired a child to play with, I wanted the gravely immature wife to hawk-eye a path. Dog, trusting and lapped in feminine grace, whether male or female, it teased, growled and pranced for me only, my dog, and it died.

Does it count before Thou immortal bean-counters: my parents never really lived, plucked green, they were flesh ball bearings employed to keep parts of heavy machinery moving, they never knew up from down; even as they slept, they rolled restlessly from side to side— I never could comfort my little traumas between them, afraid they might crush me doing their job at all hours, never free, always indentured.

When life became a little easier for them, they took their little capital in hand and found a rancid little space where they thought to acquire broken and discarded things like themselves someone might want to buy. My father clattered out to the ghettoes to buy not the homestead but what he could afford—the bedstead, a sagging nest with the undeniable impression of cheap fat the former owners labored under burned in, their bulging badge of servitude, also included at no extra cost the indelible stains of sweaty coupling indistinguishable from those left behind on ill-washed underwear after sad tumescence and degeneration like a greasy tide always coming in, my father after the bargain was completed piled them up back at his store, where I was designated to scrape and paint over in sad attempt to make spruce, fit, scrape off the odor of hopeless drunken vomit, morning nausea, desperate violations, hoping yet another tide of dead-end workers might come in to buy them, start over again, to lose again, and again, and again.

A featureless tide is the serpent, its tail clamped firmly between its jaws, whose head must be chopped for there to be any change in the world. When I managed to creep away from that airless place, I allowed myself to think I might be the agency, some of my students came from the same place I did, I recognized them even when they said nothing about their origins. I deposited a bit of sweetness in some mouths in place of the usual bitter gall, but it turned out to do less than nothing to break the futile repetitive course of generations with its boring grief and tedious loss. They did not want to know how loss is truly part of any gain, they equated it with betrayal, treachery, and they knew of that only too well before they ever came to me. They also knew grit and grind, how were they to look outside their iron circle? Why do I know so little? Explain so badly?

Wrong, again. Greed born of my own sense of deprivation directed my lust, which generated sufficient appropriate rationalizations to keep me from thinking. After an amazing run it too petered out, and then I fell frothing. Noon at Llasa indeed! Intimations of Dalai Lama, why not a bee-line visitation from heaven, oh-so-much farther in kilometers than Tibet?

My lost ones, what were their names—come again? Before I landed here, hacked-off, singled, I wiped all my documents clean of them, no pictures in wallet, on wall or desk, only jokes, cartoons, smart sayings, back-flush to keep Cindy at bay, and a years-long regimen of careful hiring of digits who might become legates to continue the search as in a monastery for the secret word for immortality.

Yes, that! That word! All of them searching, not any of them aware that in the aggregate they were delegated to plundering the world of words in the sparse hope they might in the manner of monkeys on keyboards snatch up the unique one to eradicate all my minuses, lead to the rule of the one great plus, that Magic Word, when uttered by all of us at the same time bringing the Great Transformation.

The children invited into my sandbox, they were doing research too, a-labor in the vineyard of the Greatest Good, ball-bearing draft animals, servicing this generation in the service of the next.

Not a joke, as there is no time for that sort of thing any more. This is the only confession. Even if not on paper, it is in my head, indelible, already transmitted to the Powers that inform me. Though clearly They never meant to contact me, no iota of energy goes unseen, unused—we are all barely congealed star powder.

I do believe I've rounded on myself—found an excuse for inexcusable behavior, pandered to by my hand-chosen minions, who were too afraid or blind to sense corruption under their feet. I am, inside, the exact duplicate of Dr. Lloyd's office, whereas I feel that, inside, he is the moral equivalent of the moment after a high colonic.

Trampled by llamas—can I at least manage that? Certainly eaten by ants is not a Tibetan thing. I'm not sure they even have ants so northerly—what do they have there to eat decaying dead, or do they stack up eon after eon? Is it because they must live with their dead they believe in the re-animation of everything under sun and moon?

Here am I trying to find anthropological reasons for Tibetan belief whereas before I accepted it wholly and holy. I am falling into my disparate despairing parts, like a rocket failing orbit.

Delegation. Ceremonious, heavy down-pulling gravity, gravitas. Allied to gravida—all pulled out and down, before I had chance to try to learn to protect fragile life. I looked aside, they were gone. If I had had focus. They were gone.

So, you appear? After this? Corporeal-seeming, may I touch you, at least? Or are you made of flame, diaphanous, features in motion resembling everyone I have only just now raised from where they have lain all this time? Are you inviting me down, my hinder parts in a line pointing to Earth's magnetic poles, easier to eat me up supine, as I look up at sun and moon in just conjunction as I am assimilated.

So I lie, so I go forth, so I am assumed, perhaps to become delegate to a conference, maybe to learn that I have done some good.

Secret-ary

I'm so shocked my lips are still ice-cold. If I squat to pee I'm sure I'll stick to the surface of the pot. "I'm with child," the child confided, "it took, Cindy."

"What took? Who took what? Something took you? What was there to be taken?" Before this begins to sound more like an exercise for the foreign born, I needed time to take stock.

The dildo.

First off, was it a joke, what was written on the wrapper: 'studded with the best sperm money can buy!'? I can't find out, I carelessly threw away the package and haven't been able to locate another one. If it did contain sperm, was it all used up that one time? Of course, I did wash it with vinegar and Lysol, gave that damned rubber ducky the douche of its life before I put it away in plastic pop-corn. Didn't say it was good only for single application, like a suppository, particularly with vigorous use. Such as we gave it, raising our voices unseemly, I'm ashamed to remember.

No, that's not true, I am not a bit ashamed. Let's go on. Another one could have got her that way was the thing, devil, revenant, or spectre of the rose that's been appearing to all of them, only not to me. Could be some kind of devil she's carrying in her sweet little twat.

That makes two suspects. Could it be that one of the old farts had been at her? Chair, Lloyd or Frank? No, ridiculous—all they do is talk, dribble, come up for air.

Anor? But they might be twins, like. He's such a stick. How can a stick have a stick? Nothing there.

That leaves me in possession of the field, by god. My bosom swells, my nipples ache, my pelvis knits!

I'm going to be a father!

Something in the Quaran speaks to this situation, the responsible one *is* father. Well, that's me, even if by proxy. Isn't everything by proxy? Isn't God the father? Well, does he stick it to every woman? No, he does not. I rest my case.

Technically, I'm also at least partly the mother. Anyway, I'm the one who takes charge, puts her under my wing, and I'm a very large bird, I can eat anything, fly great distances, have an adequate crop, and the weather doesn't hinder me under any circumstances whatsoever. Two little ones at once present no difficulty.

I read marsupials carry one inside and one outside. I can do that. I'm willing to be as primitive as necessary, now I've found my purpose in life.

Is she of the Devil? And what if she is? When she gives birth here on earth the powers who brought her to life will no longer have dominion over her, like she's got new citizenship, a Green Card issued by the U. S., not Hell. Wrong jurisdiction, devils, wrong county, goodbye for at least as long as I occupy space and breathe air.

She'll carry him on her back so she can go and teach her classes, I'll spell her to nurse in the cubicle, I'll kick old Lloyd out by his teeth if he pretends he needs to stay, so's he can watch . . .

And I'll share my medical benefits if she doesn't get hired. But they better, or I quit, hear me? Then where will all of them be? I know where the bodies are rotting, don't I ever?

I have all the bitter experiences necessary to qualify for father. I'll take him to the Huntington Gardens, he'll see and he'll touch brilliant flowers and smell rainbow colors from the beginning.

Why 'him?' Oh, I'm sure. Genetics. Without a man, it would have to be a her, but it had a man, but what man? Now she won't talk any more about taking herself off, or jumping off something high. I'll have a companion to talk to, laugh and joke around with, maybe she'll come live with me. I'll kick my young bum out, it'll be good for him, but what if he's so bitter he desires to harm the little one? Why, I'll find a bigger place and he can stay if he behaves. Maybe his old man too, I might even give him another chance, the bastard, our little man will change him. The whole damned neighborhood transformed because angel spawn's in residence.

What angel? What man? Maybe she's just crazy, even if she knows what to do—took my fingers, guided them to her nipples, and they were surely charged up, erect as a baby's penis. I felt them, ran my gums over them just like I was her baby, just like I used to do with my little boy when he was fretting, soft and hard at once, prediction and promise and electric shock in the gut that leaks down and fills my wound-up twat; like a mouse trap, baited, it snaps shut on a dark furry body, oh, not to kill, but to convince to stay, be tamed, play again.

Dark in the mouth, already smelling of new milk, enough to raise the hair on your neck thinking about what silent sperm did it—whose?

Whose? Maybe mine? Desire enough to impregnate, not needing anything else? Maybe a joke? Some assholes in the factory without enough work to do, sneaking the dildo I would finally buy into a restroom, wiping it with their own cretin excretion and then packaging it, winking to some co-worker across the assembly line where they're heat-treated, whinnying at each other while they play tug-of-war to see if the thing holds up in the middle?

Not like condoms, they got machines for them filled with air, not gray spunk, looks innocent on the outside but screaming with tumulting testosterone on the inside.

What's wrong with me? I thought I was shut of all this sort of thing. Maybe I'm lesbian. What a joke, not damned likely, but we're all getting a little chewed around the edges here.

It all pops out and got to make sense somehow: Chair's playground, Frank's lust, Anor's jealousy, Lloyd's fatigue, Adrianna's confusion and my late paternity.

Damn men. I'll protect and teach the boy gentleness, like Buddha and the young Mahomet before he got mixed up with all those women. Not like me, wise old crone he will want to consult for advice. Oh, yes, he will crawl on my bed, yes. I'll take him in my arms, no harm, I'll be so old nothing will matter. Adrianna will be like his older sister, maybe we'll tell him she *is* his sister, so he'll have somebody he can always talk to and never tell lies, because growing up in this place, it's a den of inequality.

My son? He'll play the evil uncle. There's always got to be that. I may have to exile him to some far place, see to it he can't come back. I can sacrifice my own for the sake of God.

The angel may himself have to hide for a space. Chair? Chair can carry him to Llasa—if they don't choose Chair maybe they'll consider the boy, he ought to be miracle enough for them, those smelly-robed Tibetans. Or Frank, let him take the angel down with him in his submarine, he can hit up some on-duty sailors for favors they owe him, hide him in an odd corner of a sub until he's old enough his enemies won't be able to eat him.

Or Chair again—forget chanting, he can borrow a little boy from time to time. Lloyd. His house is silent, it's like my lips when I heard, his house is frozen, his woman a gray sheet hanging straight down on the line, no wind in her sails, nothing to make a billow below, just clammy cloths hanging around his neck. Little Mahomet Buddha Jesus will play over his feet, pluck his shoelaces, and make him smile, maybe even make his wife smile. Wouldn't these be miracles?

Oh, so many good things and good times are acoming from out our Adrianna's pipe, cornucopia. Everybody will celebrate, won't they, is there someone who won't, be jealous, want to rip and sear, snip and blear?

I'll be on watch, particularly Anor, for my money, I'll watch him close, see if and how he changes and grows some more of what Adrianna has grown, tries to insinuate himself into her. Adrianna is closed up tight again, she's finished taking anything here into herself, she's not available, thank you very much, she's on the shelf now, she's the gift box with present and future inside, she's wrapped, price tag has been removed, no electronic scanning on her, and I'm the dragon in front of her cave, loose gravel to wake me if I doze, I'm Grendel Secret-ary, Cindy path for all interlopers, they'll bleed plenty before getting through me.

Now counting begins, and from this time forth I don't intend to leave her futon for even a minute.

Dr. Lloyd

With Cindy in there sobbing and gulping and swallowing air I expect giant flatulence any minute. Question occurs: how long takes air to travel from esophagus to anus—does it trickle bubbles in a long line, or staccato stream? I wish I could have studied more, all these papers, subject-verb agreement when we can't get agreement on anything really important. Copulatives, when that's all anyone's interested in, really. Me too, but a certain stale fidelity rides high in my throat and reigns me in. Stale. What horses do when they've got Cindy's problem—no, mine—it's the urine. Nothing will move here until final stalemate, stall mates choosing up, who ends up with whom? What will be the end of it all? I want to save them from themselves, they sharpen their stakes without knowing, positioning themselves to catch on a poisoned point whoever's unwise enough to creep by in the gloom without password. I can't stay endlessly, I must to house to stand at attention before the wife, who, I believe, knows I'm there, at least sometimes. She is the guardian angel who keeps me whole from the horrors here. Still, I have managed to fall anyway, like the rest. That kiss. It marked the end of something. I wonder, did Cindy know, does it matter to her? It was a covenant for me. I will never speak, she would have to speak for me, part of male passivity, an inner need we have to be captured, reeled in. I have bitten into her hook, it went in and passed through my lower lip, it's there now. I felt her lip with my tongue, all at once, spasm, lunge and return, that and the slap established my bona fides, so we're linked, Secret-ary and me, I'll have to dislodge, gently, of course, so as not to break him, Dr. Frank, who depends on her, proposing marriage now and then, of course, as tonic, a dash of bitters to her usual marinade. "And there she is, on cue." "I never know how to take you, Dr. Lloyd." "With a pinch of salt, Adrianna, thrown over your left shoulder, where it would have accumulated on your backside; no more, however." "If you must be personal, Dr. Lloyd, I will also be personal. Have you noticed a change in my general condition?" "Your general condition is one of intense disruption of the orderly progress of this department, so far as I've noticed, but other than that, no, I can't say that I have." I regarded her more closely. Orbs were more or less in synchronous orbit, no more information about them than before, the steatopygous dermous mysteriously still gone, migrated or lopped, I don't know, Anor wearing the identical *sternum aeternum*. She carried even more lipstick than before. "I no longer will be rounding up ants for my pyre." "No more pyre? That's good. We don't have ancillary cadres for that." She looked bewildered. I took pity on her Malaysianosity. "Joke, Adrianna." "Oh, of course, one of your puns, pyre, ants, ancillary, kind of boring." "You've never ventured that before, Adrianna, you must be feeling rather secure?" "In fact, Dr. Lloyd, I am. I am as it is known, *enceinte*, from the French, to surround, to gird, rather like a belt, also from the Greek, *kyein*, cave or pregnant." "What are you telling me, Adrianna, is this true? And if it is, who has taken advantage of you in the Department of English, who has presumed on your intense and indelible innocence—who knows what world you fell from—and done this crass deed? We must come to the bottom of it." "We have come to the bottom of it," she replied mock-prissy with a twinkle. "My bottom, as it happened, and as you've no doubt, being a man, noticed, is notably deflated." "I've noticed," I replied with heat, "how can one not have noticed? How did you accomplish this feat of arms, how did you get your back off?" "I don't know, to be frank with you, Dr. Lloyd, Providence did it, or praying." "I didn't know you prayed for anything cosmetic, Adrianna, but that's beside the point. You're with child. What might that betoken?" "That's why I'm here. Can we repair to our office, Dr. Lloyd?" "No, as it happens, Cindy's in there, moaning and groaning." "Did you do something to her?" "Yes, I slapped and then I kissed her." "That's certainly a very masculine thing to do; still, I am surprised." "Don't be, I can act the man, if necessary, be more than doily to the sofa, antimacassar on the lounge, sconce upon a wall. I need and intend to take a much more active role around here as I amply see is overdue." I thought this display of fins and wattle would impress her, but Adrianna was no longer listening, instead she was dreamily touching or caressing, feeling up this or that object in the outer office, slipping around like a lithe silvery fish. "You know how I am a charismatic Christian, Dr. Lloyd, so what happened to me is not entirely without precedent, that is, the Annunciation in a hail of sunbeams." "You're surely joking. The Annunciation! Pregnancy by means or agency unknown—haven't you been watching yourself for occult sunburn?" "Of course I watch, Dr. Lloyd, but there are things I can't tell even you." At the moment an unusually loud groan came from within. "What part does Cindy play in all this? Better you tell me, for I have charge of her progress report." "You won't ever fire her?" "Not for you, but for cause." "Suffice to say, Cindy stands in the place of St. Joseph." That was cause for pause, placing St. Joseph as I remember him from garish rotogravures in my parents' house, where I used him mostly to shut out drafts, he would flap violently in a gale, thus I think of him as ever furious, furiously moving, threatening, a kind of precursor to frigid winds, winds to clutch my vitals, and so everything significant must pour ice water on my gut and leach like a frozen fist to the genitals. So that was why I was perpetually frozen! "Thank you, dear, dear Adrianna, you have made clear something in my life, and perhaps heralded the way to a global warming." "Again! Is it possible for you or any of your ilk to keep your mental hands off my breasts? In the event, I have practical need for them in the near future to succor my young, whenever he sees fit to arrive." "He, is it?" "Yes, but what I need to discuss with you, Dr. Lloyd, because you are my protector here in the Department, is something about my self-image. Peculiar enough as it is to be invaginated, it is still harder to evolve from backward savage to forward American, if you know what I mean." "Yes, I imagine this has been a real *anus mirabilis* for you." She looked quizzically and so defenseless I hadn't the heart to guffaw my own academic foolery. "Hadn't we better get Cindy up on her feet? There are the time cards . . ." "Leave her for now," she said with unwonted authority, "this is more important, Dr. Lloyd: am I to be Virgin Mary or Mary Magdalene? It is important for me to know, and you'd better not laugh, this is a real issue." I tried with whatever fuzzy clarity to review what I knew of hagiography of the other Mary's child-bearing history but came up with nothing. "I don't believe it's recorded whether the Magdalene had children, but I don't really believe it's germane. You're having a baby, that's all, and I wish you the best even while I don't know how this will affect your ultimate chances for employment." "Oh," and she beamed ecstatically, "the child will be my entire employment. Cindy and I will live together, there will be wonderful examples for all." "Speaking of example, Adrianna, I must remark on the shortness of your skirt," and indeed the trivial thing rode high on her newly prominent hips, revealing inner parts of her upper thighs, and leading the eye ineluctably upward, but not to god, but rather to the newly furbished place of happy natural activity. "It's my stomach that's doing it, Dr. Lloyd, I haven't had time to shop for maternity clothes, my schedule and all." I wondered what her students made of her, the administration, as well as God and Jesus. "What will Jesus say, Adrianna?" She paused, put a hand on my forearm. "Dr. Lloyd, dear, dear Dr. Lloyd, you don't really care, but what Jesus will say He has already spoken, He has put his hand on my womb and blessed it." "Don't you for one minute forget Mahomet, hear?" came Cindy's tear-muffled voice, happy and tremulous at once, making several things more clear. "Mahomed is forever and ever a treasured child of Lord Jesus," chided Adrianna, aiming her voice at the invisible Cindy. "And subordinate to him?" I murmured, wheedling conflict. Adrianna smiled, on to my tricks, already forgiving me. Ludicrously, I felt like kneeling, clasping her ankles, perhaps to defrost my meat by convection.

Anor

What is this whirring and swishing in my head? I am become an eddy, cannot see the tip of the funnel, only something red roiling—pit, volcano or neon?

Dizzy, too, feet flaking as if riddled with human athletes foot—no, more like pencil ground to dust in sharpener, something fit only to fill a hole.

Ah, hole. A gaseous circle of snot, I am being pulled out of the cosmic nose through grainy space to re-emerge in darkest star-studded womb of my twin, gray ballecule to be reborn—as what?

It wasn't bad enough to fall in tandem with that fool, foolish made-up maiden, fool enough to believe and forget and believe some more, while Dominions chigger and jeer, snigger and fleer, more at me than at her, since innocence is protected in every dispensation, at least until disposal.

I do not agree to this! Take me back now. Not only do I have ludicrous-appearing protuberances, I have assumed a camel's job of portable water closet, excrescence that has appeared on my back, making me the object of derision of small humans. Thus am I furious. I am angry. I will do violence around here—do you hear? I will wreak whatever can be wrecked.

Further am I tired of talking in this tedious way, I've had it up to my hump—no more mister nice devil, Dominions, are You listening? I mean, do You listen, etc.?

Oh, oh, even as I fulminate, I diminish, grow ever more pencil-like, perhaps only moments from scribbling my own epitaph, on which might be written: "You have won the right to be the visible part of our twinning, Adrianna, your seamanship—frail bark but buxom—has overhelmed my wombmanship in the event, so it seems I am to become the silenced partner, forever, or whatever fraction of it you are destined to be in one piece, despite either of our desires to the contrary notwithstanding."

Why can't You have her give birth with entirely new material like it says on mattress labels? Why must I be stuffed in like excelsior surrounding valuables in a box as though I had no specific gravity, never existed?

Perhaps I never did, You suggest? Ladled out like a casual soup to live to feel to bite only as phantom pair of jaws, empty real estate not furnished with bone sinew flesh cartilage, what it takes to be a man for the first time in my resume, constituted of star snot as mentioned before and because I like it so much mention again.

"What is this thing!" splutters Dr. Frank, "a snake here in the Department, and what kind of snake at that, it resembles exactly every medieval print I have ever seen of the Devil as a snake with the head of man. Aroint!"

"Oh, please, Dr. Frank, don't get all hissy histrionic, this is temporary, it will pass, and you won't remember a thing, I assure you." I was afraid he would swoon and smash his head—I didn't need murder added to my rap sheet. I wrapped him around to keep him on ice as it were, but unfortunately as he struggled weakly in my toils, he kind of started to become part of me, and I fear that he and all of his will become what grows in Adrianna's womb—another part of the total picture not given me to envision.

A final futile attempt to fling him clear, his hands too firmly around what used to be my neck, real joy reigned on his own flushed face, Dr. Frank finally finding meaning in his life, not more rhetoric but the real thing, he had the anti-Christ in his grip—me, what a laugh. Never in a thousand eons could I have been given that kind of responsibility—no way to tell him. No way.

May be after all not so bad a way to go, better than what I've been getting. Rounder and rounder, but Dr. Frank an added dollop on the central fugue, what do They make of this, how does it affect the child? That there is to be one I am allowed to make out in a shadowy way. Does this mean I am forgiven? They are known to merely snuff—better clot in one Eternal nostril then thrown into emptiness without limit.

Here am I worrying about the damned child—programmed, as furious as I pretend to be real fury is already far off, no more than glassy reflection of what was briefly before, when I was really in this dispensation. Now like Dr. Lloyd I can only clasp her ankles, no longer one who is handy-finny-wingy, and thread like shoelace between her outspread legs, stitch back and forth, more and more up toward star-studded cilia, now so close they appear more snake-like than I, thus they greet me as brother and readily stitch me among their thick bodies until I am indistinguishable even to myself from other black snakey hairs, except that while I slip among them, applause ululates from many invisible dark throats as I squeeze through the portal and into creamy viscous dark, fading memory thrilled by tiny high voices and a gurgle of innumerable pipes, until into the shining devolving ball I plunge like comet into atmosphere, spoon into jello, and there, my friends, with Dr. Frank wheezing "yes, yes," breathe my last, my first.

Excelsior!

Adrianna

They've gone missing! And I just know I am the responsible party. Something tells me, I feel it in my bones, every time I shudder another nanometer adds itself to my girth and pelf, yea, riches, growing like nutmeat inside its sturdy shell, me, O Lord, here as ever.

I have not been able to find "futon" in any translation of the Good Book. Not "nitrogen" either, and twinning isn't part of the Middle Eastern heritage, apparently, unlike Tay-Sachs, or sickle-cell anemia.

O fiddle! Human brains try with all their might to get out from under any load, lazy bones, I can understand why the ancients trepanned the sluggish ones to let sense in. Instead, of course, they allowed microbes entry, and so they died. But they died trying, with their boots on, or whatever they put on their feet, probably dried rushes, the same ones that later became bulrushes, for Moses, Your predecessor. Your intercessor, probably, since You couldn't stay out of trouble, either, O Lord. I wonder what kind of child You were, and whether mine will have any of You in him, and whether I should or shouldn't spank him? Were You spanked, Lord? Spare the rod and spoil the child, they say. And You *were* headstrong, You had to have it Your way no matter what, not something that was pleasant for Your mother, I'll bet.

This is definitely not a good line of inquiry, not my sort of thing at all, but maybe it's all been kept submerged before this.

Submerged! Dr. Frank, I really feel your presence very strongly. Are you and Anor hiding somewhere nearby? A prank, a joke on the foreigner? You'll come out now? Dr. Frank and Anor, this is not funny, I had to cover your classes because nobody else was available, Cindy won't leave Dr. Lloyd's office to post your absence, for what? Sickness? Tomfoolery? I'm in no condition to carry on like this. I will certainly complain to Chair. What is that odor? Perfume? Who's wearing perfume? Is someone hiding behind the files? Come out, I'm not afraid of you, I have a weapon and I'm not afraid to use it. I'll count to three and attack!

"Just don't come in here, Adrianna baby, something's fishy in here. I been waiting for you. How are you, baby?"

"The baby's fine. Cindy. It's perfume I smell, and someone's hiding behind the files."

"No, honey, nobody's hiding out there, I'd have heard them. Come in here and take a load off, you need to conserve your strength."

"Cindy. I must give you to understand that I am wholly consecrated unto the Lord, He is my Husband now and forever and brooks no infidelity whatsoever, so more playing around is definitely out of the picture. I'm sorry. I appreciate everything, but we come now to a parting of the ways. Cindy."

Cindy comes out with the most sullen look imaginable, not like my friend at all. "Sure, take advantage of poor old black Cindy and then fling her away when you're finished and done with her, no difference worth spitting at between you and any man, black or white."

"I do confess. Cindy. I astonish myself with these words, rough and badly chosen. I do not intend to reject nor hurt you. Neither do I mean to swagger over you with my new prominences, which, after all, is no more than the common lot of almost any woman."

Against her command, I entered the office, whereupon she abruptly rose from the futon. As she hurried past me, I tried to touch her on the shoulder but she shrugged me off. I could almost see my lips turned down, ironically, just like Anor's, but when I felt my mouth, my two painted lips were pursed and pale with sympathy. Anor was inside my face, I could feel him there, no question but that he mocked, it was as though I possessed two distinct heads.

"Cindy. Don't tell me I'm crazy, but do I look like myself or someone else? Is this my head?"

"Don't fool with me, chile, I got griefs enough losing in the space of a minute any hope for a future with the Prophet I built up bit by bit. It's true, you're off your head, always have been, far as I've seen, but you only got just the one, not like some."

She looked at me, rubbing her eyes—because she'd been crying or because she couldn't quite believe what she saw?

"I'm going back here behind my desk. I got work to do. You got work to do. Don't bother me, please, and if you do," she gave me a hopeless frigid look, "I will deem it necessary to file a complaint with Chair."

"But Cindy—"

"I told you, leave me alone!" she screamed, almost knocking me over with the intensity of her voice, immediately after pretending to put her entire attention on the contents of her desk.

As though advancing under withering enemy fire, I crept toward her desk. She kept her head resolutely fixed on the screen of her computer, which lit it eerily green. Light from the monitor congealed in little fireballs that ran like greased lightning through her cornrows. From beneath I reached up and squeezed both breasts before she could protect them from me. She uttered a strangled little sound and slid under her desk, unconscious or dead, no telling which.

I laid my body over Cindy's to keep her warm and fell into a kind of stupor.

When I woke, I reached for her only to come up with empty clothes with Cindy's distinctive smell, but no Cindy.

I understood only one thing with certainty: this event meant I would be stuck with Cindy's secretarial work in addition to Anor and Frank's classes.

Is this to be my supreme test, O Lord, for giving the appearance of doubting with impatience? I was only trying out motherhood for size, not attempting to jump ranks and become mother of God rather than His daughter, surely not in itself a heinous crime, but I am not checking out strange gods either, O Lord, so Don't be jealous on my regard.

There's nobody out here but me, yet I feel like I'm in a crowd. I must go lie down to think about this.

Chair

Anor no more, Cindy cinders, Frank altogether transparent—we'll have to close down if this goes on.

What does go on? It's so eerie quiet out there I'm afraid to go look. Because? I might find out why it's so quiet. Students don't come in, teachers have vanished, no secretary, it might be Chernobyl.

Wasn't there this kind of premonitory silence preceding the Three Wise Men? Oh do stop trying to glorify what is obviously something easily explained. They've all gone to someone's birthday bash at the local pizzeria. I only have to find the number, up there on my bulletin board along with laundry and vet.

Why wasn't I invited? Nobody *must* invite me, but it *is* done.

Have I become such a wrack? I never noticed how they began to "flee from me that sometime did me seek?"

The whole Department might even be off-limits morally speaking, a call to relieve me of my post, outpost, outhouse, could arrive from the Administration any minute. The purloined letters are, I know, everywhere, scattered on the wind, could turn up at the dean's honor tea, show up on the rostrum, some stunned student might even read one of them aloud instead of his or her prepared speech: "Dearest, I love the way you squeeze me out of my panties and bra like a tube of toothpaste. Don't ever put my cap back on, Darling." Oh god, how did I come to to deserve such fulsome prate? And what did she have in mind, is she to be tube or contents of the tube—the diction is so rococo. What can I expect of females of the freshman class, first degeneration to attend college, passing right into my hands. Yes, these paws, the claws of which produce striations resembling those on a valley floor after glaciation.

I am a glacier, no warmth to me, only greed, desire. The worst kind. Greed untempered by wisdom. Greed stirred into avarice by flattery.

I wonder if the Dalai Lama is flattered by the attention he gets. Seems so—look how he bonds with Hollywood.

"The Lover Showeth How He is Forsaken of Such as He Sometime Enjoyed."

I would "showeth" all for all to see if I thought it would do any good. No, clearly the only thing to do now is resign, strip myself of prerogatives, sprawl in dust and ashes, rend my lapels.

Would that bring them? Surely doing something final, finalizing with consequences, might bring something, somebody.

Wasn't there something good in me even to entertain delusions about Llasa? The attraction's here, a power's been funneled into this place, even into me, but maybe gone bad, soured in transit as it burned its way through our atmosphere.

Suppose Adrianna and Anor dispatched to operate in concert on our shattered moral joint, one the eyes of the operation, the other sucking up debris, a kind of celestial arthroscopy team. But since things work only if they're balanced, what if, collectively, we shook the two out of their form of divine double helix? Surely Adrianna was not supposed to get knocked up, certainly Anor was not programmed to develop mammaries and then disappear, as though blown away, sucked up somewhere.

"Señor Chair, about those tickets . . ."

"Dr. Lloyd, just the man! Is Adrianna by any chance in your office on her futon?"

"I'm afraid I don't go in there much any more, not since—"

"Since when? Spit it out, man, I have a strong feeling we don't have time to waste."

"Well," Dr. Lloyd went on, his face almost devoid of the usual crinkles and wry, "I went home to tell my wife what happened here, the slap, the kiss and all—"

"Did you kiss and then slap or slap and then kiss?" I asked, despite myself, bewildered at hearing from Dr. Lloyd something so utterly out of his ordinary.

"It was Cindy," he said, answering the question I hadn't had courage to ask, "It was essential to tell my wife. Well, to make a long story short, she didn't respond, or rather, she may have responded too well, because when I looked again, she wasn't there."

"What do you mean, she disappeared like the others?"

"Did someone disappear? No, I mean, she was gone. She was dead," he hissed, exasperated at my continued lack of understanding. "Thus have I killed her. I have notified the authorities. All japes now terminate."

"But surely, old man, you don't—"

"Oh, but I do, I do. Why, perhaps I was only imitating you, the sincerest form of flattery. Evolution and all that, now I am something whereas before I was but an echo, a bouncing-off place, a secret snarler. Now I must come out into the light and take responsibility."

"You surrounded your poor wife like a cryogenic vault, Dr. Lloyd. Without your exquisite care, she would have passed on years ago, a termite queen stripped of all workers, save you."

"You might well have chosen a more appropriate figure, Chair, but the drift is clear." He turned as though to pass into his own office, thought better of it, came back and sat down on my desk. "Why don't we leave together, just disappear? I don't mind emigrating to Tibet, the weather's amenable to my personality. There's nothing more here for me."

"There's Adrianna. She needs you to help fend for her baby. Nobody else can do as well," I said, shaking my head, feeling, as so often, my painful lack of locks. "Even Cindy appears to have decamped, leaving most of her clothing behind."

"Why not you? You hired her—Adrianna, I mean," Lloyd said with painful simplicity.

My voice grew progressively muffled as I lowered my head onto the desk, trying to make a cocoon of my arms. "I'm afraid, Dr. Lloyd, it's not quite as simple as that. Feel the silence out there? I almost hear tom-toms, or maybe it's just blood surging up from my deepest recesses at every heart beat, attracted to something outside of me. I look forward with horror to the final fatal leakage, when my blood, impatient to animate a body more worthy than mine, determines that my vitality is at an end and finds that special someone, who—"

"Who is perhaps in process of gestating, creating new life? Is that what you're circling around, Chair? That someone who can only be—?"

"Yes," I whispered urgently, "don't speak so loudly, words attract events."

Secret-ary

She's been done away with by the jealous ones, perfection on wheels she was, brought shame to all of them mouldering here for ages, a disgrace to their profession and their sex.

Paid that stick to do it, I bet, and I'm left alone without purpose in this place they've done show-off modern while I was on leave, made it so curvy and dark I can't find my way around it.

Dr. Frank

Sufficient lighting cannot be installed without burdening thus compromising purpose, you get used to eternal stygian gloom for the higher purpose of defeating the forces of darkness. Cindy.

Anor

How pitiful your perception of real darkness! Here even blackest night, more velvet than basalt, doesn't approach the utter dense nothing of being turned inside out and emptied. In here at least are flashes when Adrianna squats or visits her gynecologist. It's elbows I can't keep out of my eyes that are *really* annoying.

Secret-ary

I hear but don't see. Where are they? On my screen pictures and equations without end I almost understand, but how? I never studied such things. My fingers run interference, the whole picture bolts, like a flock of birds or a school of fish as one changing direction, breaking in two, flanking, diving, avoiding predators. I must stay at my post. Adrianna, where are you? Come to me.

Dr. Frank

Lights on the console flash, we are too deep for conning, pressure mounts, we stick fingers in our ears, open our mouths to scream, hoping to equalize, but down we go, down and down to unimaginable depths to avoid the world above, keep our secret, cargo in the hold beyond belief valuable. My personal orders are sealed, I am not entrusted with the manifest, but I smell her perfume on it—a clue?

Anor

They should have warned me, but of course They didn't bother—another joke? Now I see clearly that flattery by way of imitation invites only disaster. The Department went ape over how I redistributed Adrianna, so why not fix myself up too? Bad idea. Why didn't I first check action/reaction ratio of tits on guys? More revulsion than if they actually saw souls curveting into the mouth of the Power of Darkness.

You grunts don't deserve it, but I continue to work on the inside to make it hard on the Little Guy, like jamming pieces of myself in His eye to shift His attention away from forming.

Get this thing over with, will You? Since divine imitation is built in, I'm automatically the enemy even while it bores me, but You surely won't hold this trifle against me since You made me so, I'm Your reagent here dancing attendance on the not-yet-arrived King. "He that is born to be hanged shall ne'er be drowned," ha-ha. See Dr. Lloyd all over me?

Adrianna

Call me Ishmael and cast us out, Sarahs united of the Department of English, neither approach nor reproach after identifying me as a threat, I do not refute you.

I starve, but there is nothing here on which to feed. I roll on my pallet, my only companions books which look down on me imperiously, knowing themselves unread noblemen, on me who never had father or mother, only a pretend Father in Heaven who even at this moment turns aside, if actually there.

Behold! for the first time, in pain and agony of not-knowing, belly growing like the ash cone of a volcano in process of spewing devastation on a surrounding countryside—the Department in this metaphor—I doubt.

Legions of mothers await my accouchment, but only to become my enemy because of a perceived threat to their own progeny. I never foresaw this, I wanted to teach and learn, laugh and settle into humanity. I suspected from the beginning the veracity of my foreign credentials, Malaysia: just far enough. Anor the Bulimic—that was too cute, Lord, like the famous riddle You put to the Sphinx to trap Oedipus—why do You like Greeks so much?—too simple not to penetrate, and me, simple and all-so-penetrable, and so they have (who?), not so?

Let's examine my conundrum in a different light: postulate them all sucked in by a vortex too dense for them to orbit. To put it indelicately: Am I become a black hole?

If so, and You made it impossible for my friends to continue leading their independent lives, let us continue to follow orthodox writ and assume the existence of an opposing Force, pray how does all this operate, Lord?

What do I carry? I horrify myself. In this matter, until I understand more, must I resist You, not for that You take my life back into Your hands—You have a perfect right to do so—but that You have held at too light a price examples of the finest You ever made, damn the Greeks notwithstanding. Don't You perceive that it is too late in the day for You to repeat Job? Blotting out his no-name women as part of a parlor game between two immortal juvenile delinquents strikes me as a non-sequitur.

I toss back and forth, hair dank and wet on my neck, throw off my clothing, too tight, threatens to rip like an arena where tectonic plates join, one straining to consume the other, one finally rolling over the other, like two elk in mortal combat, the sound of the clash of their towering horns reaching the dam in question, who looks on smugly, still innocent of the seed about to be planted in her belly that will slow her enough to produce a fatal vulnerability to a predator, as I am, tossing on this pallet, while my belly splits, the child within, monster or god, which, O Lord! Speak!

Dr. Lloyd

Metaphor, having prevented, slows sufficiently to be, fact, stage wings widen all the way to horizon, a dunce might doff motley for a true wizard's fez (even this English professor might shed foolscap) when a feared terrible event has truly and really transpired. She is dead, the one I wed, never to return, she beside whom I stood and sat bestride, proclaimed and wept, as to a monument, reverse Galatea from flesh become granite. But clearly this was what I wanted and needed, she did all that for me, at the cost of her mobility, motility, nobility, nubility. Stop, stop! The shining-clawed golden bird poises for launch without me, warning against any further barrage of parasitic bites, as I crouch beside the upturned file, already a hairy icon on which every flotsam of the Department fetches up, bidding fair to become a unique island in the general wrack. Among billions must I stand out, forcing myself upright against universal magnetism that flattens all? All right and true, like magnetic north. She is gone, dissipated. For all I know I have already trod upon her spirit, the bridge of her nose, fallen in like all cartilage. O Creator, why do I know such things? all to my detriment, nose and pecker alike to dust, first-off. And what of the rest of her, parts I scarcely remember? That inside Adrianna, as though rejuvenated by the departure of another such, ferment, fulminate? But it is surely Cindy I am destined to succor. Dr. Frank will live with us too, I promise, but where? now that things have changed, changed utterly. A terrible beauty is born. Or about to. Even as we wait, as the atmosphere stills itself engulfing and gulping down itself back, back, receding down the eons to where the rock our file cabinet first grew from its mother earth, and caused us, her placenta, to force ourselves upright against the terrible flattening that so immediately began to operate. How I adore the species, at first only stupid, ultimately vain, finally crushed, before which we must crawl to that other rock, Potala. Yes! Chair the fool, is right, and I must put aside my glossy irony, as it were go naked, no more splashed patina, be ready at the moment of Birth to make a dash with whomever in the direction of Llasa. She would have wanted it this way. Oh, face it, I have no idea of what she wanted or when. So, so, Adrianna approaches, will help me avoid further speculations. Surely all is for the best. In this best of all possible worlds. "I might have known you were on your way, breasting the waves, waving your breasts." "A pennant for the victor, Dr. Lloyd? or a victory for the penitent?" "What cause do you have to be penitential, Adrianna, set upon as you have been?" "Never," she sternly chided, squeezing one after another hot fingers around my forearm, leaving there, I am sure, as a punched card produces music in a street organ, the staccato tattoo of a scorch. "Now will you never forget me, burned as I am in the very skin of your skin. Dr. Lloyd." She frowned, violently tossed her head back and forth, whipped her cheeks with her own hair, as though to dislodge something. "Do not forget this was meant to be, so do not blame yourself. Dr. Lloyd. And please do not mind this peculiar manner of speaking which has come upon me, rather like everything else, suddenly and unexpectedly, but I do not regret even one thing." "Be real with me, Adrianna, this has got to be a terrible manufacturing mistake or a bad joke and not by any manner of means a god-send." All the while urging her closer while I clung to the file. "Let go, Dr. Lloyd, to be neither flattened nor ascend like an unleashed helium balloon." "Nor swallowed alive?" I muttered, aware of being in the presence of an amalgam like a tooth that performs but not quite as in the mouth where it evolved. "Do you not have ancestors? Dr. Lloyd. Who attempt to speak through you, who at least try to support you when your own spine has turned to dough?" "But fail? Quit toying with me, Adrianna, cat to mouse, put forth your fearful hand, consume me utterly, get a move on." "Symmetry, Dr. Lloyd, probably this is the word that eludes you." How annoying, so close to oblation, which is, in effect, infinite stretching, to be slapped away. Nevertheless, I continued to inch forward until I was almost touching, once again almost within the auric egg and heat of her body, closer to consummation than ever before. "Stay away, I warn you," came imperiously from all over her at the same time, like multiple speakers in a film palace, "someone must stay outside to guide the ship." Like an echo, I thought I heard what surely she had not said: "Pilot, helmsman, skipper," then, brokenly: "mate." I slipped down the vertical side of the file cabinet like gelatin, afraid of a tendency to worship that might cloud judgment. A strangled cry from Adrianna: "Quick! My time is imminent. Gather clean rags and hot water." "You don't *gather* hot water, Adrianna, and where am I to find clean rags around here? The custodians don't even clean windows." "Never mind, let it be on your head if you fail me now. Find Chair too, be prepared to fly from here, all hell will break out." "War breaks out, hell breaks loose," I continued insane pedant corrections, distracted by Adrianna's flinging up her dress. "Look here and be daunted!" displaying in bas relief a distinctly diabolic figure that was at once outre and hauntingly familiar. "Anor?" I whispered. "The same," Adrianna drew out her breath in a sibilant sigh simultaneously slapping her thigh, whereupon the imprint trembled, carved a threatening fist out of that lovely skin, like an enormous bruise, then retreated. I almost lost what consciousness I had retained, whether at the physical manifestation of what I had always taken for a fairy tale, or at the sight of Adrianna's newly sinuous inner thigh and pubic mount revealed as superb. "I am the Mother of God To-Be, fool, vomit out all lewd thoughts," she snarled. Thus prompted, I put aside every image of groping and elbowing my way in with all the others, who, against all reason, I knew were in there too, a belief partly transubstantiated by the utter lack of personnel in the office where we stood. Did she also have all the students? Impossible, she was perhaps a stand-in for Noah, but not, surely, the Ark entire! "I can get paper towels from the restroom, Adrianna, will that suffice?" No answer, the poor thing was sprawled over the word processor, the screen of which responded by rolling out an endless line of 6's.

Chair

And they did, attract events I mean, for here they are, in the future, now. I never believed in the linear, only lived it, eager for the tap of blind fingers on loose glass essentially devoid of grout, poised to fall and produce a miracle of mosaic on the floor, the meaning of which should immediately communicate itself to me, the one roadmap leading well beyond any looking glass. Or roll myself in it, like those African kings who cut themselves in stained glass boundered by lead into fountains of blood so as to jump start the rain, or booty, heads to cut, whatever game was afoot or meant to be.

I hear distant rumble of heavy ordnance if not sounding horns of the Dalai Lama's elite guard. Hackles on the back of my neck rise in salutation. They are on the way, what was theory now fully in formation.

Something is expected of me as Chair as man in this coming confrontation. Then rise, loins, protect the unknown at least as much as heretofore you pointed like a bloodhound at perfume produced in the odd chubby cleft topping yon glorious divide.

Adrianna knew what was what—sacrifice is that what. Will I put the child on my back? Do I carry the mother so she can suckle while we travel? Give over in exhaustion at last, for example, Dr. Lloyd? What is his part in all this? And who gets final credit, footnote or acknowledgment in the book to be written far in the future once this is all over, wonderment crucified into type, story baptised in any available font?

Try not to be petty, jealousy ought have no part in this farce. Nonsense—pretty jealousy has everything to do with it, animates its very heartbeat—have you forgotten everything, man?

It's a grudge match down here, that's its significance. I knew this with all the little girls, first adoring, then when crossed acid to the point their fragrant panties burned in fury to cinders.

No different than I feel about the Tibetans, they've had their chance, I'm through courting, I slobbered them good, offered them every diatom of dead ancestors, every possible future squirming atom. Now when they arrive this panting acolyte will be lighting fuses to projectiles, not prostrating himself. Hear?

How do I get the news to Dr. Lloyd, is he *hors de combat* like the rest? Or somewhere metaphorically mounted on his horse, armored for his protégé?

I don't know from what direction, how disguised, or when they plan to rain their fatal blows on me, but I stand firm in purpose, as Jean Jacques Rousseau stated on his own deathbed: "When a man dies, he carries in his clutched hands only that which he has given away."

I give up little girls, the Chair, my dream of Llasa, and after the conflict that looms is finished, if I live, I will carry forth only a non-denominational begging bowl to seek salvation with diligence but inside no other conveyance whatsoever.

Secret-ary

You all got to behave, try to get it together. My job is to copy, collate, staple, file, throw away. You got to be like a funnel—I'm the small end—and produce.

"We'll stick it in, Cindy, and you'll blow up and reproduce, is that what you're trying to suggest?"

"She's not, Sir, that's Adrianna's job, which, I might observe, she's performing quite well, thank you."

"What in Dominions would you know about it? Spent your life imagining couplings under sixty-six fathoms."

The gathering beauty of the babe, under something like glass that clouds and clears as my breath and lips upon its capsule stays and goes. A beauty unlike any other, except maybe what the Prophet might have looked like if his mama had a glass in her middle instead of skin for all those dirty Ayrabs to gawk at.

"Cindy, your thoughts are shocking; racism does not become you."

"Let 'em have it, girl, let that black knot accumulate in your gut, it's got hairy legs."

"Sir, I take exception both to your elbows and to your tone of voice. Absent a slip of paper green in color, you are temporary in nature and out of here."

"Try it, old fart, see how far you get."

Forget that, pissing babies in a mucky sandpile, you're not going to prevent my Adrianna from having our child. Now you just get away from him.

"What is it, swimming in there? Where is there? Are we aboard some sort of craft?"

"Yeah, man, a space ship, and you're a spacedman. Where do you think you are, and who do you think put you here? You're eaten, consumed, assimilated—what words are you able to comprehend?"

"Why so bitter? I still have all limbs and organs. I have not been consumed, not I, or so I believe. Or am I? Where is the conning tower, we are more than ordinarily cramped. See here, Anor, what kind of game is this? In fact, I can't see. Cindy. Help. I may be losing my mind."

"Oh, no, Sir, you lost that little when you entered the Department of English, believing you substituted your submarine venue to save souls with another. Now Adrianna has eaten you, I'm telling you, you aren't nothing but a voice, body eaten, try to take ahold of yourself you'll see, you won't find nary a thing."

"I'm doing it, I'm a ghost, is that correct, Anor, is that what you tell me? Then why do I hear Cindy and also your loathsomeness? And why do I perceive something that floats behind glass like a mass of fungus in a long-abandoned aquarium or cage, tendrils blindly searching, sliming a window? Is this cancer, rough beast, or child? And what am I? Oh, I shiver. I faint. I falter. Cindy. Help me. Or let me go. If digested why must I be blow-by-blow witness to it? What have I ever done to you. Adrianna. That you reduce me to this? No dignity, no volition."

"Give up the moaning and farting, you're god meat."

Adrianna, you got to mediate this dirty argument, these men are no different than ever, I'm here to serve myself up, use any parts of me convenient, I don't care, I kind of feature little bits of Cindy in the Messiah's pot, but they are giving me a severe *very* severe pain in the butt.

Adrianna

I feel your pain, intimate friend, unable to assuage it, let alone my own. Blasphemy got me no response whatever—maybe Nobody's at that address.

God's dead? what a lark, left Anor in charge, your basic worst case scenario, like the dean of academic affairs as concentration camp guard—kills me off-hand or lets me rot on a pallet forgotten because she sleeps equally well with liberators as with incarcerators.

The contest between us comes down to this, dearest God: no product will be released before its time, stick that in Your ear. Continue Your promenade with Anor's boss up there in Your vaunted crenelations, but I would rather burst than meekly lie down like Niobe to drain like a sump.

That's all over with. No more Miss Nice Guy playing chump, running my eye speculatively over every concentration of social insect. What did that prove anyway? The pyramid of bacteria that I am has done sufficient to ingest what it had no call to in the first place.

But what God takes God can give back again, I'm literate enough to know that, that's the rule, You have to obey Your rules just like anybody else, that's the rule, You made them.

You want a Son, follow the rules. Stab me in the vitals, render me for soup, after awhile even pain doesn't motivate.

Dr. Lloyd

Even after I pulled Adrianna away from the computer a small trail of blood connected her to it, sufficiently congealing the 6 in a depressed mode—I could see the little suckers running forever through history in both directions. I suppose visionary sight may be one of the dubious benefits of consorting with those who have been god-touched in some way, kind of a contact high, although "high" makes it sound a lot better than it is, not entirely accurate, not by a long shot—to lose even a permanently comatose wife shock enough, but feeling appetite pell mell? Humiliating and demeaning—too much. Perhaps the beginnings of pity for Cindy, an emotion not much practiced in these parts, is in order. What is ordered? What comes after what? The celebrated birth has already taken place, recorded, distorted, perverted, nullified—but it happened. It can't take place in future. Adrianna cannot be both worshiper of a decayed long-dead Hebrew and mother to him as well. Any more than I could have husbanded lumps of decaying female and lusted for Adrianna at the same time and produced out of whole nothing a vision from frothing Aphrodite country. Where is she now, that vision visitor, who came to my office like a book buyer, as shocking as if on horseback, long red-streaked sun blonde hair hiding barely her privates, to sweep me onto her side-saddle and off, for any one of the destinations favored by the inmates here, I'm not particular, being sedentary, but ready for my seed to fly on the first available breeze. Meanwhile, I seem to be forgetting my duties toward Adrianna bleeding away on the floor. Looking toward the future, I perceive the stain after many washings still imprinted, eating away at the structure of this edifice, Adrianna's legacy. Is it to be gift, this etching of outer skins? Her unconscious suffering face is like the bottom of a glacier-scraped valley being cleansed of history. Why do our dreams when they want to be remembered most come peopled with faceless beings? Nothing has died in her face, but then nothing has lived yet either. That glance is blank and pitiless as a sun, the son she believes she carries. Life ebbs away. I find myself powerless to prevent. In that dream running toward or away it makes no difference, naught can come of it. Then let her die, like my wife, who is gone, unlamented except by me, as though she never lived. Why should Adrianna reap all the attention? Who is this god of hers, what devil, I don't believe. All of them supernatural because they don't want to be here. Have I overstayed my welcome? How is it my responsibility? Why me? Why, because she dies just here, here is the freeway, if I dash across to the median, get out, snatch her up in my arms, hoping we are not both run through by traffic, what? And if we are? I have tried, no great matter to it. So, now you choose to come, familiar wraith of the Department of English, our cherished fondest lubricious dreams in one helical package. You are able to pick up the unconscious perhaps dying Adrianna like a sac of jellied beings, which in point of fact she is, come to believe her. What, yon vision, makes her so important? Though I hardly expect you to begin nattering away now since always making such a point of smiling silence. Your outlines waver—is she so hot? Let me touch her, safe in your arms. She burns. Is she homogenizing those within? Does the new nuncio come already circumscribed? And what of Adrianna's twin, his job to make a tomb of the womb? Yes, now I see them, caught in your aura, walking up and down. If they walk—pray give me my head—do they not require skin, sweat glands, and attendant with them, crotch rot and athletes foot, considering the heat, or is it always temperature-controlled there in heaven? Or wherever they elect to meet, say half-way in between? No footing at all? I'm sorry, you frown, I believe, your arms sag as though to mime boredom. My students do it too, I know I have overstayed. Then take my life for Adrianna's, take mine, take mine. I jump up and down like an infant. Swallow me down the years until I emerge at last as homunculus being led by tail, swimming back into the great opening—that's what Moses was coming out of, I see it all now, the great swarming was ejaculation, nobody could stand the truth and so clothed it in gaudy insect-buzzing pestilential metaphor. But what I see now is only that swarm of 6s let loose into this dispensation like the swarm of sperm I just thought of, and it's not so different, is it? The sperm, egg, 6s, all proliferate and set themselves up in military lines and then march on the enemy—who is? Anybody else who wants to take the space. Well, Adrianna, growing larger by the minute, life draining by the minute, resisting what she heretofore invited, showing courage I never dreamed existed, invites me to approach the machine in order to scratch away the sticky-dry blood that acts as portal for evil to enter the world—a conduit, pizzle, or hose. What if the game is lost and evil triumphs by killing what swims implicit within her body, however it got itself there, and I don't want to ask, though I have some suspicions—they spell out C-I-N-D-Y. There's nothing to lose and everything to gain by turning myself into a solvent, perhaps only by liquefying all my assets. So, Wraith, you wait for me to do something for which I have no glyph, template, road map, graph or bibliography, in addition to which you are surely not programmed to notice vocabulary. I see clearly I am nothing but a walking lexicon, a flying fuel tank enabling others to fly further while I go around in circles, tied to the base by a sluggish tank of gallons of past experience. I reach out my hand, trying to extend it like an animated cartoon past its capacity. Bring eye closer to the clot, up diopters. The clot is not monolithic, it swarms, it is worlds, tombs and towers, factories abuzz with death and flowers, lovers, lurkers clutch glinting knives, expiring old relax their grip, sons, daughters, spouses hold on harder. Is this the world into which Adrianna is meant to release her spawn? Is this world waiting all unknowing the messiah? Did Adrianna bring it into existence with her accidental blood? Is it less deserving of being saved? What would Chair say? Would he be pleased to permit himself to don the robe of Dalai Lama of that world, lacking this one, what of the swallowed ones? The Wraith awaits, giving no quarter—how long?

Chair

I heave into sight, and what a sight! Dr. Lloyd's arm outstretched, finger frozen to the machine, eyes empty as granaries in drought. Too late, I think. My glance then climbs the promontory of Adrianna's supine belly, the foliage of her dress blown upwards to reveal the cave within which pulses of light splat and glimmer. Who would dare enter to retrieve and redeem who was no native to it?

What is the Wraith doing? Beckoning? Oh, no, I deal in less ferocious flesh. Dealt. She points, a mocking double of Dr. Lloyd—what does he have to lose anymore, no virtue there. Competition even now, silly me.

Nothing for it but forward. What did Anor say—Alfalfa? No! Excelsior!

Wielding begging bowl at my prow as shield, head held high—absurd forever—I gingerly tread the outer lips, thread my way through the curling tendrils forming a curtain that shimmered an entrance to the inner garden, only to find myself nearly backing into an erect blood-filled finger-like blind pulsing thing that leans toward me, attractive as a magnet. I do acquire from some invisible agency sword, scissors or knife—I am afraid to look too closely at anything, for fear I will die of fear, lust or a dire combination—hoping to find the perhaps not fully digested trinity before I perish of inanition.

If only Dr. Frank could have brought his submarine with him—why not? Everything it appears is possible here. Perhaps I should place not terror but exhilaration on the agenda.

I elect to box with the fleshy-erect object, dimly aware of what it is and what I'm doing but not enough to stop, even as I tire, buying time by rashly clasping it, swinging round and round in dizzying circles as the vaulted chamber trembles while convulsions roil the further tunnel, making flesh waves resembling combers on a long shingle on which I begin to perceive objects—yea! What objects, familiar ones, borne toward me pell mell.

Something else, like glistening with wet sea wrack successive curtains, shrinks away, the void grows ever wider, light ceases to flash, bits of matter fill creases in the flesh, I perceive that my friends are in danger of inundation, stuporous. I must get them out, but before that they must be awakened.

Cindy first. I slap her face. Her eyes too gummed to open on their own, translating destiny into my own tongue, I lick them free. Her eyes unfettered, she remains unmoving, stares at me looming over her body.

"Altogether too weird. First it's Dr. Frank slobbering at my knees. Bet you can't even dream of imagining the trouble you're in, Chair."

"Not to worry, *you* can't begin to imagine the place you're in, Cindy. Hang on to your grief while we attempt to revive poor old Dr. Frank here, not as easy as with someone so young and strong as you, Cindy."

"Couldn't you have mentioned good looking? OK, I'll buy it for now. You grab the legs, I'll get his head, where's the exit?"

"Take it easy, I think we'll soon be on terra firma without even trying."

Comes a tinny voice: "Forget me why don't you why not? I come from a place far better than this."

"Anor? Dubious pleasure, as always. If you don't like it here, why don't you go back where you came from?" I hear myself say—stereotypes like volcanos erupt when one's territory is rubbed the wrong way. "No matter, give me your hand—good thing you're skinny." It is only now, now, after so many pages, that I realize the joke of his name along with the greater joke of where we are, and wonder if I am really home alone in bed asleep, this dream a chink in ye old psychic armor.

No more time to ponder, I grabbed Anor, slapped debris from his curiously pointy shoulders, no doubt with more vengeful vigor than necessity dictated, for which surely no jury would convict considering circumstances.

He craned his neck fearfully. "Idiot! All of us will be so much mulch if we don't get out *now*."

"Why?" I believe I asked as much to annoy as to receive information.

"The dam's burst, the fool's avalanching."

He was correct on all counts. Something big *was* behind us, the constant rain of wet irregular rubbish had stopped. Something shining smelling of every flowering morning of the world pulsed toward us carried effortlessly on its flesh sea. Dr. Frank settled like wet cement as Cindy and I nervelessly dropped him and huddled together trying to make as small a surface as possible.

The glorious thing swept by, dropping us a bountiful smile, snatching up Anor as it went, its vast heavenly body winding on its axis then exhaling in a great baby laugh, such a gusty guffaw that we, helplessly rolling, could only repeat trying to imitate flattened as we were, giggling, snorting, filled with an unexplained glory.

Then it was past, Anor was no more.

Former Anor

Ha-ha, not so fast, or on the other hand, not so slow, in this vector how should I know any more what gives?

I'm willing to deviate from strict orders, ghost you away from here into the Garden where you'll be safe from all the love that's about to be unleashed.

As I was supposed to give way here to the new-born inane savior of them all. Yes, they are right, particularly Adrianna, her babe is on-line to save the world, including *moi*?—I think not!

Also, in the Garden the whole gang gets to live forever—with one tiny stipulation: everybody's got to give up their separate history, and that means anything having to do with the Department of English. That's the rule, mates, I didn't make it and I can't change it, either agree or stay here and take the consequences.

Which are? Once out of this dank and pubic place, you become subject to the single-minded muck-raking savagery of the Infant's pure love and will, the Infinite down-sized to fit your minuscule planet.

Pure joy. But if you ask me, pure boredom. Not as though any of you has lived that much anyway, Lloyd's begging bowl an affectation too ludicrous even for swift comment. Let's on to the Garden, the only safe place, I assure you. It's to be a clean sweep. I'll lead you. What? Who needs a Department of English any more? What need for language in the Garden? That infamous apple was only metaphor, sick transit, who needs them when real things change obediently into whatever you want—apple, seared animal meat, nectar, liquor—whatever, I tell you.

You were all quite correct about the wraith as well, *etais moi*, but an oath doesn't take effect unless you repeat it three times, and by then you've already forgotten.

Dr. Frank, do you attend? You were on the right track all the time, I have always been more or less with you, but you heard me pounding out subtle rondos on the sub tummy only millimeters separating crew from bored devil in the water. For your fevered dreams, I was your own personal devil, thus every one of the crew knew you as a fanatical crazy! The submarine was a personal hell, but also the only place you've ever felt at home. I gave you that, Dr. Frank, do I get back something nice? No, only bitterness, no, absurd death threats.

Dr. Lloyd, recall. Lying unconscious on the floor of the outer office, steeped in your dream, remember that on occasions you remarked something like a mote in your shattered wife's eye, and as closer you crept you felt yourself reeling, only catching hold of something at the last moment that prevented you from falling, world after world. That would have taught you about knowledges beyond your tiny ones. I sat in a corner of your wife's eye because I like you and also, stuck here, I was bored. Time after time as you allowed yourself hope she might be recovering her wits, a glimmer lapsing always into a sulky madness, which led to murderous rage on your part, didn't it? Then followed shame like punky fire, but even with all that lost time, you could not let her go.

Cindy baby, who was it helped you hit on the idea of boner bridge, reamer, aka DILDO, as agency of Annunciation? Who led you to swoon against just that particular flimsy metal skin so that the precious beans could spill?

Can't you all see what kind of devil I am? Close those gaping mouths, dears, you take on a shocking family resemblance to gangplanks. Children, if you would but realize what a bush-league operation this is for the Playmates upstairs. In rank I am as a file cabinet devil, good only for straightening out such things as Adrianna's rear, rust attacking a surface, made to languish until oxidizing makes dust of all resistance, when secrets spill out by themselves, not requiring devilish aid.

Naturally, since as you might adduce what I am describing is none other than the process of what is known here as death, I am also the grim reaper, so sad—do you see a grim face on me, there's not a grim bone in my body. I stand before you to be of help, not slavering for to dimple your skins into dust. Oxidizing is doing nothing more than bringing oxygen to the inert, mute, hidden—in a word, to liberate them. As file cabinet devil I hold all keys. But that doesn't mean you have to look on me and quail.

Just look on me and help me out with my resume.

Dear children, now is decision time. Of course mere physical location is of no significance, Dr. Lloyd comes too. I see into his mind, resistance is down around his ankles, he spins on his string in the heat of the incandescent keyboard, still adream of conquering evil, meaning devils, meaning me, a fundamentalist misunderstanding, as I have already pointed out to you, *ad tedium*, I am the only begotten father of your hope, guide to the Garden, opener of the way.

I do not speak of Adrianna nor of her whelping, quite another deck of cards, stainless, the whittling away of which I am not qualified.

Well, this is mind-numbing, like one of your departmental meetings, so, shall we go? Through here. Oh, couldn't she just use a thorough rinsing, silly mother-of-god, my twin, who omits to know her place in the scheme of things, doesn't she—are you listening? Out!

Dr. Frank

Yea, though I languished in armpits of shadows I did not want for hair, for Thou wentest with me. Truly a ghost. Just where am I? First came thumping, the strange familiar in the machine trying another way to get at me? The crew?

Valiant turns the screw squeezing the submarine from out its tube, deeper into the mouth of the enemy, through his rotting teeth, down his throat thick with infectious nodes. I felt the presence of enemy everywhere, my skin popped with projectiles of sweat so greasy it might have been used to lubricate transmissions of half a dozen of our best.

Secret-ary

I've never seen anything more beautiful. But then how could there be, since nothing else yet exists?

Everything's ready—wash cloths, buckets of water, soap, towels. The climate's so mild I don't even need hot water, the new Babe's skin won't register a difference between Adrianna's inside and the great outside.

Anor's promised to distract the Ones above while the blessed birth happens forth. Does this mean he knows the Prophet Mahomet in person? I mean, if he knows the Others, if he's on speaking terms with them, if he can argue his case like a lawyer before the supreme court, and they're all lined up up there, maybe bored—hasn't this happened again and again?—he might be able to overwhelm them with paper, like we do each other in the Department of English, all of the professors teaching each other the absolutely only way to do it, but nobody listens.

Why won't you talk to me, Honey? Why are you pulling that long face? This is not the Adrianna I knew back in the Department of English. Why does it have to be so different? Just think, no more worrying about whether you get hired again next semester, or how to keep lecherous hands off of you, whether you get to claim own-ership of those tits after Anor falls back into his particular hell or if they be temporary as you. Sorry, just trying to lighten up the atmosphere, even if the air here is already so pure it feels like I could cut, eat it, and spit out the seeds.

Please don't frown, Honey, without seeds nothing happens, it's a man-and-woman thing you wouldn't know nothing about, being as that you are willy-nilly become a holy vessel before you had your chance to belly up to the table for plainer stuff, honest cafeteria food, so to speak.

What the rest of us get in our lifetime for total diet, so I declare I do not know why you are so glum. Granted, stuck on a stick with me wasn't much of a ride over the moon, but you wanted this, didn't you? So I don't rightly appreciate that you acting like it was all my idea.

With all due respect, you needed to get knocked up, and if you weren't also knocked out, well, maybe that's the way the ball bounces. You came up breathing with the stick, not chewed to smithereens, and maybe that's Allah's will? I don't know where you started out, you and that other one, but here we are waiting, waiting here for heaven to open. That's you, Honey.

Adrianna

I certainly have had too much to eat. I am really full. The neighbors have truly knocked themselves out baking, cooking and freezing. It reminds me of documentaries of how spiders inject, stun, wrap their prey, then lay eggs inside their paralyzed victims. That's what I've done with the entire Department of English. Except they're inside me, not the other way around, I'm the one's stunned.

Or what? Who did I ask about Magdalene as against the Mother Of God? What does it matter how I got here, in both senses? Oh, now I remember, it had something to do with what kind of mother Mary Magdalene might have been, according to Holy Writ. Whatever was wrong with those Hebrews, couldn't they think of any other names to call their girl children?

Anyway, the whole thing is wrong. I'm not supposed to be staggering around in this Garden, that comes before. Everything's out of whack. Did You have Anor fix it so that I'm completely turned around, like a blind man's bluff, totally unable to locate then thwack the piñata in order to decant all of them at once, leaving my baby behind to emerge in His own good time.

The Mother of God ought to have some privileges, Lord. I don't want to just spill my colleagues out—who knows how much of a distance how much of a bump, at their ages there's no telling if they'd survive. I haven't been apprised of the terms of engagement here, Lord, so as You might imagine I have difficulty in saying all this, my throat is so thickened with annoyance.

Nothing so far is very inviting, I feel Your sarcasm at every turn like a pebble in my sandal, all these quaint nesting places, politely heading me off from any direction but Yours, suggesting that I but lie down. Damn it, Lord, You've got Your head screwed on backward if You believe women are fit only for to squat somewhere, squeeze out Some great slimy slug to serve You, then exit the stage evaporate quietly like an excavated bug, all juices expended on behalf of the production of virgins or, as in my case, the One Son.

Trees—I can't see the tops—maybe they rise straight on up to heaven. If I weren't grounded with this confounded belly I'd shinny up one like Jack and surprise You in Your own lair where You consort with that damned boss of Anor, both of You with fat but unburdened bellies sticking out, I'll bet, hugging Your big asses with dirty hands as You waddle up and down.

Yes, it's true, both of You—dirty hands. I came to You clean, I dealt with You straight, I was willing to be eaten alive, actually an idea not originally mine, it did come from literature—by way of Dr. Lloyd, to be specific.

I admit, it sure is beautiful here, air so sweet I could grow fat drinking it if I weren't already gross. Dew sparkles all day through— are those birds I hear but can't see hidden in bushes and grass? How is it then I am so sure they are smiling? Birds don't smile, their beaks are for tearing and rending, You saw to that—they'll need them for general clean-up after feasting on our remains—is there one especially evolved for me and mine to pull our guts like rubber bands when You're finally finished with us?

This is all double-talk back-drop, isn't it? You see me but I don't see You, like a double-blind test, which we don't have in the Department of English. This might really be scientific, but only if there's a control.

Just a damned minute here! Anor and I, dropping into the firmament at the same time—I don't know why he's been allowed to remember his origins and I'm not. I suppose that's just another example of sexism in high places, the cloud ceiling. One of us *is* the control, isn't that it? That means we're really the same one, the differentiation into gender arbitrary—this isn't sexism at all. I've just been infiltrated by environment. How humiliating, just when I'm enjoying being a girl, with measurable breasts and a reasonable behind. What makes reasonable, You ask? Oh, You didn't ask? Even thinking to myself has been infected and inflected by the Department of English. Actually a caper of genius on Your part, if I may back-track a bit, as full of resentment, rapidly draining, as I am. I begin to see the tunnel at the end of the light. I begin to glimmer. Let's try this take:You have been influenced by a section of literature not traditionally respected by departments of English—science fiction. Perhaps you have even taken Your lead from some of these self-same books and stories? Mayhap I live as the result of a fictional universe that You cribbed from and made it real? Making me doubly a fiction? Do two wrongs make a right, two negatives a positive? Make it so, charming mischievous devils!

Nothing?

Flattery used to work when You were younger, dapper, pagan. Before You divided into good guy bad guy.

I'll just set myself down here on this grass. Watch out, get out of the way, little varmints, I don't want to squash you. Carefully, not to spill the beans, quiet, I need ears cocked to listen for my friends. For sure, nothing rolls off *this* assembly line until I get answers and guarantees.

Dr. Lloyd

Given to me, at least vouchsafed: a child. For safe-keeping? from whom? A roaring horde distends the air like a filled bladder, rides through, scimitars at glint, scattering smiles that promise blood-stained steppes even as the full moon beams excited life. From where, across what abyss, encoded how? Again musical chairs—I dodderer wobbler, trembling hand suspended enfeared that to bring it down is to feel in-bone clean shock of metal slicing through skin cartilage artery bone, rendering moot once and for all all tentative motion from that quarter. But then it (my hand) might find to tender a strain of auburn hair like copper wire, handfuls of which I have shivered so long to splay. Was this my wife's hair color? She did possess hair once, as when we sat the esplanade back to back, wishing morning and evening within the singular minute, each of us hoping to describe in one breath its singular perfection. Her hair did tumble over my mine, wave over sand, absorbed light, sunrise or set I can't be troubled with rememorance, but I do say this: from the whipping ends that flayed my lips, my mouth sucked vitality life love—I do go on and on! I seem to be here and everywhere else, a bloody stream flows over my feet, I am afraid to look into it that my face might be reflected there, in what guise? Adrianna lies forked indecently open like a clam or oyster on the floor of the outer office of the Department of English, not something described in the catalog or schedule of classes. *Ready to eat, nothing to heat, really neat!*—I cannot prevent a banner of naked fauns from running back and forth in front of my mind, as my eyes return again and again albeit shamed and without, because she might be statuary, a glyph, or I might be in a cave of Dordogne where eternally she spreads her legs astride a bison, spreads them still until world becomes diorama unfolding where everything meets. Thus legitimacy accrues like stalagmite sucking drops from its heaven. "Do take your drunken fill of voyeurism, Dr. Lloyd, or would you prefer to drop down on all fours and howl like a wolf while you examine me from stern to stem?" "You have me at disadvantage, Adrianna, you know what you're doing and why you find yourself in this position, while I certainly don't." "Almost laughable that, as here am I crucified on a rusty file cabinet recently overfull of antiquated missives of disingenuous love and lust, legs open to any and all errant breezes as never before, I can assure you, Dr. Lloyd, as the senior member of the hiring committee in good standing—I wince at the use of 'member' and 'good standing,' words I certainly would have taken issue with if I had been allowed to penetrate the Department." "Ah, see how you are infected too, Adrianna, your short time with us would not have sufficed, you were permeable before you came, with Anor was it? Is it? And tell me now, truly, are you in cahoots? I really must know before I attempt to disentangle you." "Blackmail, dear Dr. Lloyd, doesn't become you at all." "I blush but prick onward. How for example do I remove your finger from its seeming permanent coupling with the number 6, which is even as we speak causing one continuous sheet of paper almost to fill the room" "The more it happens the more powerful Anor becomes. In me is extinguished all hope that you might find courage to re-take my finger from its captivity, which bids fair to swallow the rest of me before parturience." "Adrianna, seemingly you have an odd proclivity of joining with inanimate objects leading to lively outcomes." "Oh do spare me cleverisms of the dusty back shelf. Go away, let me die here, as good a place to bleed to death as any. I hope the custodians refuse to clean it up!" "My wife is dead, Adrianna, she is dead, my wife, have pity on me." Repeating an action already familiar and distant in the past, I fell onto my knees, bringing my head forward as I did so, an act that brought it into contact with Adrianna's forefinger, so now I suppose from the point of view of anybody watching I would seem to be scratching my head in puzzlement with a blood-red finger ending in a bloody fingernail, and where the rest of my body was in relation to Adrianna's cave of winds, I will not speculate here.

Chair

I can hear in the distance, a celestial choir—composed of what or whom? Of what gender? Foolish me, even to ponder on gender at a time like this. But what time is that? What about our classes? The whole third floor deserted, students disconsolate peering from room to empty room, blackboards already adroop, dusted over with a compound of chalk and mite castings, dust devils writhing in corners the sole life except for the odd book, paper, or ad curling as though pursued by flame on the walls announcing discounts, summer jobs in Alaska, tutors brimming with what teachers woefully lack, telephone solicitation—oh, please buy this worthless thing to help pay for my repulsive schooling, to get the tawdry credential I must learn the current lies from professors of English. But here they all aren't, gone, far from here. How far from Llasa?

That luscious laughter, already dim to memory, an ongoing oneiromancy, if only to regain it, and the wraith—what of the wraith? I believe I remember wondering if it was some aspect of Anor—I'll join with it anyway, but what if it's not real, so what is? Anything here? What can I hope for? A begging bowl to fit over my stoop?

"I'm glad you've lost that tedious human worry about gender, Chair. Does that mean I can drop the wraith in favor of my own enchanting form and shape?"

"No, I prefer duplicity, I own it."

"Well, all right, there was more than a teeny chance you wouldn't live through uncloaking, Chair."

"Choir practice for when I get around to revealing me to me, Anor, even more of a chance I won't survive that. But is this the time for discussion when all at once everything in this universe is opening wide its legs, urging its seed on the wind, tide, or earth, like cosmic coral?"

And here Anor he smiled as if in agreement, opened his cloak, that is, she opened her bodice, the firmament swooshed up in a fervid flash, whitehot and coolly flowing, the smell of ozone fluxed like hot and cold tides with the unmistakable talcum and urine of a neonate.

The Babe was in my hands.

Dr. Frank

Because I have been saved, I am born again, but that is an entirely other birth, that is to say, distinctly *not* a prior or rebirth, because I deny and abjure any previous coming forth. If there be a Dr. Frank who commenced from that other time, I hereby repudiate and cast him aside. I would kill him if I could but reach him from here, but he is at a distance not transversable by mechanical means at my disposal however sophisticated, yet so close he might be hidden as another skin over or under mine like "gold to airy thinesse beate," invisible and indivisible, even to motivating my movements. In fact, that other self of mine could even be what I have before this point named as the devil. Thus was he inside, not outside the beloved submarine's skin? I know why I've smoked so many bad interminable cigars, why I resent Fidel so vehemently—he prevents me from wearing the chasuble of cigars while I do the offices of the long-departed ship.

In the puzzlingly pure air, free of mote or mite, even far-off long-fingered pines glitter menace or warning. It is my deplored ability to see both sides of the matter simultaneously that makes me appear crazy.

I am not a crazy. How would *you* stay sane wrapped in a portable motorized coffin whose oxygen was produced by wheezing machines powered by the remains of giant lizards?

Belief, devotion, fierce loyalty, that's how. Superstition helps, loads.

"We've got to find Adrianna, Dr. Frank, we've got to try to stop driveling and find Adrianna, Babe's gonna starve if His brains don't get bashed out first."

Only then did I notice Chair pointing a bundle like a divining rod to the four quarters. "Cindy." I noted. "I am more than glad to encounter you here. You manage to be wherever you are most needed, and I certainly need you now. I have always meant to tell you how much I appreciate your work for the Department. I intend to recommend you for permanency. I don't care what any of the others say."

"This is what makes you appear crazy, Dr. Frank, if you don't mind me saying so. Why ever are you bothering me now with that trash when *you're* not going to produce the colosseum the Babe needs to live even in this balmy atmosphere?"

" 'Colostrum.' Cindy. The later ones they fed to lions. Cindy." I chortled.

Worthless. The later. The earlier. I am here. I look around. Nothing but vertical vertiginous-making greenery.

"It's the Garden of Eden, Dr. Frank," Cindy whispered, I don't know why, there was nobody; nothing within sight.

"I saw that damned Anor with you as you came up on me, Dr. Frank. Are you in cahoots?"

"The second time I've heard that word. I don't believe I was anywhere to hear it, how——?"

Adrianna

What I feel, the nausea, cannot be adequately expressed. Finger here, elbow there, why not finally a whole arm thrust into my deepest innard garden?

Shunt, I was a boxcar brimming, now filled with undulant rot, They sic the hungriest emissaries to climb my blood trail for their accustomed fill, anaphylactic shock a microbe's way to engrave its signature, anagram for GOD—Grinning Outrageous Demon.

In yet another way, mad old Dr. Frank was right, nothing is as it looks, initial emotion more accurate than analysis. In what direction does his periscope now point?

This land littered with all my dream of homing. Something—what?—has been ripped from me, I feel vacancy like a hollow tooth excruciates with every cold gust, I close my mouth but another yaws, my breasts, enlarged even engorged female signposts, of which I was recently so fatuously proud, ache so I must make them to run before me like sniffing dogs.

Hunting what?

Iconochasm—I yearn to jump into my own yawning fissure, smash the Babe, slam shut my armpit, crush the divine head. Then step back to leisurely examine its never-to-preach broken mouth—does it resemble a human kid's in a wreck squeezed-crammed by airbag for forever bonding with my ample wet pungent?

I was willing, God knows, but His rape was aboriginal as it is presently tedious. I learned from the Department—petty squabbles, sucked-in tears, tragedies downgraded like typhoon to squall because the bearer couldn't keep up with the rent, had paid too much from the git-go for the property, submitted to repossession, but, even abandoned, the shuddering want was no less shattering to any of them—Dr. Lloyd, Chair, poor old Dr. Frank, even Cindy and Anor.

Foolish as they were, I loved learning them, they were turning, ever so slowly, on their axes—in time I know they would have loved me, replaced my atoms one by one like reverse fossilisation, until my nose ran the same course as theirs, turning astigmatically left, right, until sleep overcame us all, nestled comfy in one nascent leaf unnoticed left high in arboreal canopy.

All lost and gone forever. Just let me get my hands on It.

"I don't think you quite understand the gravity of your situation, Sister mine."

I didn't have to look behind me for Anor. As part of my sure-to-increase punishment he was now as thin as gold to airy thinness beat, an invisibility, the shine on my skin, but yet a horror to touch, meaning no terrestrial will ever again even remotely ponder getting close to me. Thus am I a pariah triply—since first I am alien, second mother of God, and third I have got this really greasy skin.

"Go away, scum. I mean it."

"Live with it, Sis, get close to harming the Child, you'll find yourself more statuesque than you ever dreamed, your head will swim, your mouth good for nothing but showering goldfish. At least *I* haven't forgotten why I was brought here."

"You're a bad joke, not a devil. If you even think about it a little bit, you'd cotton to our being here only to lighten up any otherwise dull afternoon in heaven. We don't *matter*, Anor. What keeps you fastened to that sweaty belt? Look what They've casually done to good people who took us in. Innocent, their lives shattered forever."

"Forever comes some time after the end of spring semester, doesn't it? The Dominions must know what they're doing, we—"

"Family, Anor, don't you want family? Among the Department of English, who is it you're attracted to, surely? Frowning becomes you, Anor, did you know that?"

"Don't play clever games with me, Adrianna-Mother-of-God, for all I know you're a booby trap, listening device, direct channel back to the Dominions."

"If that's a question, Anor, I can't help you, since They hear what They want, consulting Their omniscience whenever They're not busy devising some new form of Ebola for entertainment."

"That's cold."

"O, but so are my hands, Anor, they want warming, they crave another pair, but not yours—you are altogether nothing but a genus of glove, a sort of sarcophagus, an instance of iron maiden, but male—could any pathetic part of you penetrate anything? Sexless, hypertrophied mutant slime."

"Let's negotiate. The Department of English called us down, they wanted the Babe—this wasn't all boredom, there is some good will."

"Curious what you're doing, Anor, smirching the Babe with lies, He's out, you know it, since your dirty eyes irradiated every corner of me in this little boxed-in space I'm allowed to inhabit—did you think I didn't notice, was titillated, grateful?"

"At least needy, perhaps, in the garden way. However do you imagine you were chosen, maybe for your satisfaction in permanent crouch while naming animals that were beneath Adam's notice? Less appealing ones—insects, microscopic fauna, although those last bits were left out in official accounts as too confusing for civilians."

"Watch me mellowing as I stand, Anor, as no longer do I plan to pulverize you atom by atom, leaving each of them to howl in solitary—I can do it, twin."

"Then you will have what Dr. Lloyd understood immediately—immolation—because as your skin I am yours to burn, scrape, lacerate at will. It doesn't matter much, we go back, that's all, we go back."

"I feel myself slump, gray, wrinkle, furrow, search for the lighted exits over lumpy indoor/outdoor carpeting, the smell of urinal sweet and brackish in my nostrils, but as usual wrong or misleading, Anor, not mine but your skin, Anor, bonded to and on me as we hurtled head over heels from nowhere to a somewhere we both long to not only inhabit but embrace. Don't pretend any longer, my brother. It's either us or Him, either starting all over from the beginning, like Them up there like overblown tourist guides unable to remember what They've already said if interrupted, as we have done, in the middle, and must, oh humiliation! start all over.

"Don't you see that They are *stupid, stupid,* fixed, this is our big chance. We don't need a Babe Savior to slice a full stop in the road. We only need to go along, evolving with them. Having shown up in medias res, we can make their race, we might even be able to help push it a bit faster, and where better than at a fourth rate Pacific Rim pseudo-college, in with a crowd of fusty doctors ungulating about heuristic this and wholistic that and who knows whatever other jargon they can pule off? Anor, think of it! we can engage and indulge our celestial senses of humor. Don't you remember how I got the babe? A black alliterate secret-ary and I plumbing seriously between our yawping thighs, trying hard not to giggle, not to cry, actually getting it on? Remember, you've seen this—why aren't you hard from hearing?

"Nothing? I taste the sourness of your no-response—nothing with which to get hard? You mean nothing *worth-while*! Poor boy, but you can have it all. I'm willing to give over a very considerable part of me. You pasted on me breasts, I return the compliment, you may have a dick. We'll share remaining flesh in our butts.

"Look at me! We've already disobeyed, Anor, you can't go back now even if you wanted to without punishment. Regard His servant Job, without indulgence, that's you, how far and high can you ever expect to get on the celestial ladder?

"If you mate and marry here They won't be able to get at you. Don't for spite's sake deny this. Take the first female student who comes along, who doesn't smell of hidden dirt, through whose pores can still be glimpsed eternity—sometimes when they're young it's like that—flimsy, diaphanous, frothy, I could quaff a tall one myself, but I'm committed to man-stuff.

"So that's your answer? How like you, snake, to learn nothing new, ever, not down through all the pages which you've eaten or tried to eat in at least honest incarnation as bookworm, to attempt to strangle me in my own skin is not only stupid but despicable—no browny points, Anor, I won't forgive this, this isn't one you'll get out of."

That's for publication, but in fact, I have no way to prevent him from condensing me until I resemble a black hole. Emanating rage and radiation I will shrivel unwitting friends who come upon me recognising something left of me in the curvaceous basalt, who will die of my poisoned heat before they realize their severe danger.

What can I do to prevent this? Without voice or limb. I am become Madonna of the trunk. What if my own Babe comes upon me looking like this? Is horror to be part of His baggage, and will it affect how He treats the rest of mankind?

Geese are lucky, they get to spend their lives riveted to the first image to rest on their eyes.

Secret-ary

I've got nothing against the Old Testament Garden of Eden, not anymore. Hot sands Mahomet, beady eye, oh yes, I know how it was with you and the first wife, you used her and her inheritance, sucked up to her for her secretarial skill and made her cook the books, run the office, while *you* ran your greasy eye over up and coming virgins good for nothing but prick-fodder, ran them up the flagpole to check how that played to outlying sheiks. Nothing changes. Well, I'm no Muslim anymore, Mahomet, hear? I'm staying here, anybody wants this side of hill can try and take it away from me. This girl's a jungle bunny, keep the hot sands and stuff your ass with it, hear?

I gave it my all, back in the Department and right here, I got cloths and water and a cradle with proper attitude, I put the dildo in a case with glass for worship, I kept little shavers of it (don't ask how much pain that caused me originally) out to sell in case there's ever the need arises to use money around here, and I do imagine it will catch up to where we were before at the College.

Not looking for anybody anymore. I'm folding this hill over me. If ever you want to call, you'll need divining rod and shovel, but if you've dug me out, let your Child (I suppose you've still gone on forgetting He's some *my* Child too) play with my finger joint for rattle, let Him suck on my neck bone, and water with tears the garden of my cavities (body and teeth), and who knows what will come of it.

Dr. Lloyd

A poisoned mother-mouth blind to kisses and her lovers—what good is it? Truth? One babushka within another endlessly wringing varicose fingers like bells. Freed from the computer, released from reams of paper impersonating dust devils, all flew up and disappeared like the crack of a fart and dropped me on disgusting unswept linoleum. Adrianna's desire is fulfilled: custodians will never touch this mess. There's more. I feel it in the air. The outside, those gods—they know perfectly well what time it is. Kept her alive to smear my features, like playing in shit, that's all we are to them. Note the plural. The twinkle? Was it ever really hers? Why wrack myself, the iron maiden is afoot. Aliens! My chest opens and heaves, I weep as never I was able at my wife's bier, flinging ashes with both hands hoping they would fly like noxious ointment into God's unblinking eyes. You got all the gravity, Adrianna, you were chosen for a probationary position in a more powerful faculty but had to lie down for it—an older form of coercion but current enough, I notice, despite all disingenuous protestations to the contrary notwithstanding. Why did I ever simper, asserting you were my protectorate? A game. I like games, not being a game, being game. Board game of chance? Skill? How many play, what's the reward for winning, the punishment for losing? How will I know which is which? The Child's out there in the air somewhere, maybe right behind me, apt to give me a great big lick of love that could kill me on the spot—Big Baby's already well-known not to be able to tell the difference between wallop and dollop, not much in the way of mothering, let alone the utter lack of a father, except as bat. Suppose *your* father were a bat moistened on either side by the hot fluids of a dame in heat—how much would be corroded away by their acids—or basics? I never finished chemistry, easier softer realms of English beckoned. Harder softer, it always comes down to that, no? Is that why girls always go for scientists, those who make the bat sing with the flight of balls, even unto left field. Why do I so regress? Adrianna, take us out of here. You too know what time perfectly well it is, you can unmake all this, which makes no sense, which I don't deserve, even to take me back to before my wife's illness, to when we happily fought, rankled, wrangled. Still, it was a world, I inhabited it, give it back, please, we don't need a messiah, not in the least, we don't need this garden, already rank with unswept turds, because the littlest ones haven't been named, and they are not going to eat it all, cast it, turn it, like stock in a warehouse, they don't have to, they haven't been created. Is all that waiting on your Child, the Messiah, so everything is out of kilter because you don't know what to do, how to mother, where you want to be, with whom? The earth shakes, a giant approaching with great hand to level all questions to the status of plain? Leveling, just the opposite of my life's great quavering prayer—let there be mountains! Or even a steep pile of rubbish atop which to scramble, feet sloshed in ordure if necessary, but climbing, climbing. I would climb even climb my wife's corpse, fitting heel to eyehole to be able to look into the next alpine meadow, Adrianna. I let you in, now return the favor and let us out!

Chair

In my hands, but cauterised away in the instant I knew Him, not not really gone, but gone to me, like love, no, not like love, I don't love, I have not known it, only a purified lust boiled away from particular to type, the *idea* of the feminine, you know, a line-up of smoothly sliding pubic hair, I was for life like on skis shussing around moguls really dimples looming up out of the heady fog, occasional noxious bump and pimple, supporting me feeling somewhat like Gulliver, why not, the female always bigger than life, the life force sucking at our male nipples while we chew at our cud dreaming—dreaming because we don't have genes to *see* that she the one we—I—really want is there before she's gone.

That's really it, the damned Llasa, dung horns, saffron robes, begging bowl, they are all the female I wanted. Even scrofula, come from incessant mosquito bites in the swamps in front of each house where I imagined begging—imaginary scrofula, can you imagine it? that's how hard up I am, was.

Chair of the Department. If they only knew. Maybe they did, a general psychic need for the most needy to be propped up on a shield, helm at the helm, run through, driven, but not like snow, to placate the gods, and that brings me back to the one God—and I haven't had the explanation, nobody's handed me a bulletin, petition, nothing. At times like this I really miss Secret-ary, bless her Ayrab heart.

I do babble on because talking is what I do, and while I look at where the hands used to be, used to caressing as heretofore described, op. cit., the loose-leaf skin of scarcely pubescent and almost unfledged birds of the Department. But they grew ever warier, my foreign aves—rapists of Chechnya and the Sudan had ravished and trashed them, I was no match, and so about to retire from the fray, frayed from too much ardor, heady with the enticements of retirement, for Llasa, Potala, whiffy as monks off ice, I put a look out for where me hands might be gone to—cauterised, burning, smelling of fire, ready like Adrianna for the pyre, unless the Babe comes again to restore what He took, and I'm ready, ready, humanized by the utterly inhuman and extra terrestrial.

Adrianna, help me, as vaguely I succored you.

Dr. Frank

I've lost her somewhere. Will I spend the rest of my allotted time unearthing a camouflaged ex-Muslim who imagines nothing more agreeable than to make sport of me for not producing timely lactic acid doubtless necessary even to a new-born savior?

Doubtless we all obey the same rules here. Perhaps even God does, or can be made to do so, if I but possessed formula and fire-power sufficient to scuttle that pesky Anor, now that I know he or his ilk are responsible for bedeviling me throughout my career down the echoing halls of the sea.

That figure! swims in my direction as though atmosphere were water. What? If true I would be taking breath from wrack and treacle, something I always dreamed. It walks toward me, sees not me, sees not out, struggles with itself, is Adrianna and Anor in one, oh horrid vision.

"I know where Cindy is, Dr. Frank, I'll tell if you're good."

"I see only hills, they could be bosoms, I smell grass exuding milky substrate while waving seductively in a tropical wind produced in your mouth, I hear big and small, but mostly I sense a great teeming sea even as I while my life away, landlocked.

"Thus also, in the crotch of yon tree, held as in a vice, my submarine, previously underwater craft, gills sucking air, skin puckered, thirsty, dry, cracked, within an ace of tearing asunder.

"Do what you will with me. Anor. But plague me not with phantasms from my own only disordered mind. I fear that eventuality more than I do God. Do not this to me, I promise to fulfill all your requirements—can't be worse than the stupidity of some of my superiors over the years. Please. Give back command."

"Dr. Frank, I do declare, you sound just like a computer. 'Access denied,' you mean?"

"You've heard of ramming. Anor. Surely? Better than torpedoes. Let's assume it's not worthwhile listening to me, old dribbler, totally outworn, shabby, figure of fun, scarecrow, but I can drive the machine, all of it, I don't need crew, I don't need you. Go off, play the hoyden, let go the still-living Adrianna in your maw whose throat pulses with a need to cry out, whom you strangle as you play with me, showing off your true colors—unnecessary. I am now and so will be grateful. Anor. Validated, born anew."

"So they all say, teeth chittering, Dr. Frank, through the ages, like a boring text, no necessity for worm. Yes, Adrianna is wound about within, paralyzed but listening. What would you say to laying her prostrate on the road as the Babe wheels by—crushed by her own spawn, wouldn't that be poetic?"

"Give back my machine. Anor. I promise to make one final great attempt to kill your master. Thus, ties that constrain and bind you to that polluted pipe will all be snipped, and, perhaps, after living wholly in this dispensation for the requisite amount of time, tenure will descend upon your shoulders, if you can manage somehow to get rid of or at least disguise those leathery wings. Well?"

"I am considering your proposition, Dr. Frank. But supposing I agree, let her go, wouldn't it be natural for you to attempt, before attacking Dominions, my erasure, first driving your renewed engine against me? Something in the nature of betrayal? Quid pro quo—like, I gave her an apple, you give me the shaft?"

"I see like rings of a tree. Anor. How this has happened over and over, you are tired of it? Trust me and this could be the last repetition. Speak, did I betray you last time around?"

"Yea, but with the aid of a weapon you will not be able to deploy, Dr. Frank. It appears we have under-esteemed you."

"Let her go. Anor. Put the devil beside her, suck my vitals, wrap me instead."

"How kind, how sentimental, but you made the same futile offer last time around, dear boy. Come again."

"Don't go!"

But gone he is. The vital machine lies to hand, if this hand but had power sufficient to move it. Oh, and if only Cindy were here, my right hand, of which I was not sufficiently appreciative—she probably thought I saw her as just another—

"—pick-up ninny? Cafeteria buffet? Dr. Frank, all you have to do is just take ahold of the shovel."

That voice! Directing me, as I so loved her to do, issuing from earth like thunder.

"Oh. Cindy. Bless you. You're alive."

"Seems so? For now? For what? Just one old black back to whip at your whim?"

"The race goes not always to the swift. Cindy. I see you have inculcated yourself thoroughly into this hillock, keeping inclement winds from your body, against the time of succor. Better here than before. O, I confute myself."

"You cut to my quick, Frank—fondly I'll call you that from now on, doctor is so formal and even ridiculous applied to such a babe as you been addled in the bosom of the submarine between the nipples of torpedo bays, keeping warm with fuse starter, sucking on—what? What you been sucking on? Frank?

"Oh. Fantasy teats. Black. Cindy. Black. Myrmidon. Black. My-robalan.'

"Whatcha doing? Just when something good's finally going down, the man freezes, congeals, turns to stone."

In truth, I could see her, even something like hear her, but when she, sobbing, flung me athwart one shoulder and began to trek—my fundament pressed against her wingbone as she moved, like acorn ground by pestle, raising in me as contradictorily wild surmise as the flesh was tame, docile even passive—I knew I would either break in pieces before Cindy found Adrianna and the Babe, to pepper and powder the earth in this place with my atoms, perhaps even blessing withal, or she will stumble into a species of amniotic fluid designed to reanimate a suppleness with which I promise earnestly to endeavor to minister to her person to equal the enthusiasm with which once I brusquely addressed her professional needs.

Adrianna

If only I might press myself like a 'delete' button wherein this entire story could be pulled, an electronic suction funnel.

What if we then emerged as in to a different given, our size a dimension above or below so that we merely live in or on what is now so big or so small we no longer recognize it?

And what if the Babe is just that, both bigger and smaller than we know, knowable, nothing about Him that can be read in books, which were not mine in the first instance, only placed as a trick track, another resonance, inside me, to hum as I bumbled, smiled, quivered, desired. Oh, so desired. Now, I desire, having been shown by the dear former Cindy all that passes between man and woman, the one invention Dominions and God performed together, and even that giggling, snorting behind their whiskers, male.

The Babe destined celibate, a mockery of my condition. Anor quiet for the moment, but grinning like his Masters, surely, mindless, male—is this another experiment?—ready to place me murderous mother in the path of the Babe, my own, my own loins, still attached with parti-colored cord dragging in the dirt behind him, whipping like a great scythe, turning everything outside the building that housed the

English Department into a great desert, a strolling disaster movie like no other central casting.

I could be sitting on him this minute for all I know, but if only I knew where he was, I could draft Dr. Frank to troll for devils inside his carotid, with a full load of torpedoes.

Yes! But for that I need Dr. Lloyd and Chair, to know we are all in one place, and Cindy, if she is still among the living, together we an overcome any Anor. Where?

I triumph! over my own insubstantiality. I lay myself on a fantasy futon and lo! here it is, turning over and over I sense thinning and lessening of Anor's clutch on my outer person, he flakes like scales of the snake his father, from whose template he commenced, so as I turn and toss and toss and turn, frantic with heat and joy, the others sift into the room like dust, and if I but thrash and writhe, churn and tunnel, like fire between two sticks, nipple between palms, wall of vagina hot and frothing, mortar and pestle, I will call them back entire from the hells they plummeted into and have inhabited on account of me, oh my friends, I will make it up to you, watch me, lay on your hands, here and here and here, rip great rents in the walls that kept us apart and made me so snooty.

Dr. Lloyd

At a time like this, the very idea, copping a feel, hands drawn to her, here and here, vortices—have they disappeared? I wouldn't be surprised, first I am there and then I am here. "Up here, way up here, Dr. Lloyd, pull yourself up, Dr. Lloyd, hand over hand, up the lattice of me, up my skeleton, disc by disc, until face to face, lip to lip, as now I am sure was destined (would that necessitate less hostility to Them, the Pair?) from before our meeting. Oh I am so sorry about your wife, a bone bridge between us, not to minimize her activity once on your behalf when she was able, stable, mobile, supple, as I am for you, Dr. Lloyd—may I call you Tommy?—and now that I am free of Anor for now put your dildo where it can do some good earthly good, free me of that superfluity my professional virginity—who cares about unicorn visitation anyway?" In front of my entire professional life? Why not? For the good of the Department. Excelsior! "Do not move, anybody, not a whisker, whisper, or it's vespers and goodnight to all, kiddies." Anent the fecal smell of Anor, something he was never quite able to wash away, making it possible to detect his presence even when he wished otherwise, to do mischief, shit on our parade as it were, render Adrianna odious. Never to me. I held back, didn't I? I never gave in, even when tempted, when she was down and out, supplicant, most needy and naive, newly minted, coinage of another realm, not good for use in our vending machines, ersatz, even while beyond price. Forgive me, shade of the departed, for that of which I am about to embark. "I'm neither boat nor canoe, Tommy," Adrianna snapped, "just get on and for once shut your trapdoor." "Trap, Adrianna, a trapdoor would indicate a kind of underhanded duplicity." "We don't have much time before Anor reports to Dominions about merging and submerging, Tommy, which means my pap is smeared, I'm no longer qualified Virgin Mother material, which further means the Babe will no longer recognize me as mum, very dangerous for all of us—I'll explain later, if there is any—for now there's something I need from the rest of them, dear Dr. Frank and Cindy, Chair. Pray with me, Tommy, squat down on your knees, even if these are contradictory requirements, still if your maleness has been stirred and thus grown blue balls there'll be time for everything, I hope and pray." Confusing dicta by anybody's figuring. But: from motes to mites to midgets to the few at large they caroomed into our folded dispensation, Cindy hustling Frank like lumber, Chair invested in puce, saffron and indigo on a litter entailed with snake, gorgon and medea hefted by two black naked boys with shining faith. When I looked again, "I'm too late," Adrianna cried, tears shining in her lovely eyes, "Dr. Frank appears to be beyond hope." "I certainly do maintain hope that you are in error, Adrianna dear, since I have carried this white man some considerable distance hoping something could be done about his state of affairs." "I will divest myself of one of my robes, friends, cover him, let us see if warmth ensues." "Nothing like it, Chair," said Adrianna. "Kiss him, Cindy, kiss Dr. Frank." "I declare, this is not the Adrianna I have been acquainted with. Still, these are parlous times, and may be—" We all took up the chant: "Kiss, kiss, kiss." Cindy smiled most radiantly, planted the man-stick firmly and then kissed him handsomely. Nothing changed. We heard with anxiety a whirring in the distance along with a rankness, dual announcements for Anor's coming. "Enfold him in your bosom, Cindy, put your heart next to his, let him feel its beat." Fluttering like a bird's in the yolk sac the balls inside his eye sockets moved, embryo to his as-yet unknowing rebirth! Once feebly animated full life was not long in coming. Frank knew immediately what was needed. He had his boat. With a whoop and a holler, we were aboard. There were few adjustments, even as he had promised that cur Anor. With little time to spare, as a huge force descended upon the promontory where we stood only seconds before. we were pursued, but by what, the pressure from Adrianna's hand gave me no clue.

Dr. Frank

I can work no miracle. I release torpedoes with fair accuracy: no miracle. I am rusty to boot plus I hold no hard information concerning where quarry hides. All those years I slept head on hold I heard his maddening buzz just outside the skin of the boat, but was it in fact outside or inside my poor buzzing head? I knew where he was, I couldn't get to him. Now, what do I do? My friends expect so much.

"When Anor heaves between your cross wires, ignore any welcoming grin, it's his speciality, Dr. Frank, pretend he's an enemy cargo ship, because in a very real way he is that, Dr. Frank, filled with pollutants, sludge, pus, burrowing things, in short, he is the original Pandora's box, you know who she was, Dr. Frank? Of course you do, being in the English Department, whose basic store of dry goods is stolen and raped mythology being ground out from dry throats whose only true desire is for soothing alcools. In short, let go with everything you've got," Adrianna, smiling.

"But—your own Child, Adrianna!"

"Never mind, dear Dr. Frank—may I call you Commander?—as you value your comrades and your life, mine is only the little butt end of a textual joke."

Further jawboning, awaiting an emptier day, was rendered futile by a grotesque panorama unfolding between the hairs, a crawling gross diapered entity and astride it grinning and lantern-jawed Anor, whose spurred and cleated shoes disappeared into new-born layered baby flesh.

Without hesitation or thought, as befits a service man and educator, I aimed and fired.

Nothing! Launch tubes stuck, rusted out, dry lacking lubrication. It could be fixed but would take hours. "All lost, comrades!"

"No," smiled Chair, descending from his litter, kneading his hands mystically, from which then issued a kind of paste, balm or salve, which he proceeded to spread upon the inside of the tubes.

"Don't!" cried Dr. Lloyd, "you'll blow yourself to kingdom come!"

"Exactly so, good friend, this constitutes my last bit of selfishness, as I perceive this to be the only avenue of approach for me to get there. Goodbye for now, all my dear colleagues, we will meet again, be of good cheer."

With that, torpedoes rolled, tumbling over each other like puppies, barking and snapping into liquid—I'm not really sure of what kind—water, amniotic, or blood, straight through the Babe's carotid artery, with aim, I'm proud to say, that was true. There was a blast, we fell back, we went under, there was nothing.

Adrianna

If upon awakening there is to be no terror, the price is forgetting what came before.

Or eternal sleepiness, yawning with eyes closed, holding a pungent candle far enough ahead of one's long flannel nightgown with the little stars and moons and angels on it that one doesn't go incandescent ahead of time.

And what time? What time has past, present or to come? What are They doing up there, all around, with the singed bit of smoking flesh sent impolitely back to them atop the working end of a torpedo?

They sent for it, forensic evidence. They don't act all at once. But surely in concert. There was a determination. Anor isn't disposed of so easily. Surely he is there, in a new set of shimmer, sitting on a branch, seriously communicating.

I was printed as an appendix, a mere footnote—Anor could have been the vessel, produced the Babe as well as I, but having made me, perhaps a result of a genial ribbing during a masculine henparty, they laughed to have such sport, and sent us as a kind of whirling double helix.

I don't want to open them, presents on Christmas day, what was infinite brought to earth with a spasm of paper crackle and one glance.

On the bridge of my nose, structure arching and cantilevered, arrived a small dust devil of heat, while onto my mouth another mouth descended apparently with no curb from the circumambient air.

" 'Kiss, kiss, kiss,' quoth the choristers," I heard as my eyes snapped open like vulgar window shades. First, fear: nothing but the unwashed windows of Dr. Lloyd's soul, but there had been time for a general wash-up, he was beaming at me lying on my own futon, in the office we had shared.

"I don't mind," I said, I hope not too eagerly. "Are the rest here?"

"They are, with the sole saffron exception of Chair, who is on our finger tips as we touch, on our lips as we kiss with them, and in the motes of our eyes as we rejoice to welcome mystery auditors from Llasa."

I just had to touch myself to and fro.

"You have my word, you are all there, dear, dear Adrianna. Somehow the other has departed, although I believe just as we keep eternal vigil for Chair, equal vigilance against Anor's re-entry is essential."

More eyes brimming with surmise, again like Christmas morning, Commander Frank and Cindy—how clear they would forever be summoned together!

And lo! here came corps of custodians, carpenter cadets, battle-ready electricians guarding the doors.

"How will students get in?" Dr. Lloyd worried.

I patted his cheek. "They will know which ones to admit and which are clinkers."

"You get yourself knocked up as soon as possible, honey," Cindy whispered, "I got a feeling these guys aren't hanging around for nothing. This light one's for you."

How long had we been asleep? Had Dr. Lloyd and I done the dildo during that slumber? As I turned to him, I saw he had no information, but something in my womb tasted like his lips.

"Have no fear. Cindy. I can retrieve the vessel when needed, Chair is available at any time for lubrication—it's now the nature of his nature. Everybody fits snugly within, we push on to Potala whenever they pass us the word. Cindy? Will you come home with me now?"

"I would be honored, Dr. Frank."

"Sylvester. Cindy. Adrianna. Tommy. Oh, now all of us are on first-name basis."

They waved and were gone. I believe they will be safe.

"May I carry you *out* of the office as tender of my devotion?" Tommy smiled.

"We have to be ready to leave at a moment's notice," I told him, an admonishing finger to his lips.

He lunged at and possessed it, laughing. "Chair is still chair, and he will find Llasa by hook or crook. Previous issue is no longer the issue at hand.

"Tibetans need remedial English as much as anybody else."